Donald Ray Schwartz has published nearly 200 works, including essays, articles, reviews and criticisms, a novella, and non-fiction works. *Lillian Russell: A Bio-Bibliography*, in collaboration with Anne Bowbeer, is considered the definitive resource on the late 19th and early 20th centuries' chanteuse and a significant contribution to that period of American theater in general. *Noah's Ark: An Annotated Encyclopedia of All the Animal Species in the Hebrew Bible* was the Jewish Book Club selection of the month in the year it was published and is still considered the definitive resource for that subject.

His play, *Review*, won the Sarasota (Florida) Theatre National Playwriting Contest. His epic poem, *The Cross-Country Run of Jennifer X Dreifus*, won the Mellen National Epic Poetry Contest. He won the second-place award in the New York Metropolitan Screenwriting Contest for *The Prosecutor's Witness*. His sabbatical monograph about Philo Farnsworth's invention of television, published by CCBC, is available online as an e-book, and now in print form from Amazon. His other books of fiction include a character as memoir, *Hearts*, and a science-fiction novel in collaboration with Steven Evans, *Deeptide...Vents of Fire*.

Professor Schwartz has directed or produced over 40 main stage productions, including full stage musicals. He has directed television commercials. He has featured cameo roles in two independent major motion pictures. He was a featured performer for Nebraska public television's industrial film series.

Professor Schwartz was appointed a judge for the Miss Teen America (Nebraska) for 4 years; he currently has been appointed a judge for the Baltimore Playwrights Festival Contest.

Donald Ray Schwartz is associate professor of speech, theatre, and mass communication {Motion Pictures} (retired) at CCBC (Community College of Baltimore County). His graduated students that he coached acting (stage and screen) are now successfully pursuing their careers in New York, Los Angeles, and national touring companies.

Donald Ray Schwartz resides in Baltimore County, Maryland, with his wife, Ann.

Dedicated to Ann Kibel Schwartz, with whom I have shared an amazing journey for over half a century. To our children and grandchildren—Rabbi Doctor Marcus Mordecai Schwartz and Rabbi Esther Reed; Isaac, Sammy, and Jonah Reed-Schwartz. And in memory, my loving parents, Selma and Herman Schwartz, and my parents-in-law, Isaac and Jeannette Kibel, all of whom knew and know the strength and power that results when families stay together. *Dor l'dor b'rachem* (From generation to generation may they be blessed).

Donald Ray Schwartz

THE CROSS-COUNTRY JOURNEY OF MAISHE ROSSTEIN

AUSTIN MACAULEY PUBLISHERS™

LONDON · CAMBRIDGE · NEW YORK · SHARJAH

Ordering Information
Quantity sales: Special discounts are available on quantity purchases by corporations, associations, and others. For details, contact the publisher at the address below.

Publisher's Cataloging-in-Publication data
Schwartz, Donald Ray
The Cross-Country Journey of Maishe Rosstein

ISBN 9781643789682 (Paperback)
ISBN 9781643789675 (Hardback)
ISBN 9781645365778 (ePub e-book)

Library of Congress Control Number: 2020908964

www.austinmacauley.com/us

First Published (2020)
Austin Macauley Publishers LLC
40 Wall Street, 28th Floor
New York, NY 10005
USA

mail-usa@austinmacauley.com
+1 (646) 5125767

To my production coordinator and the staff of most accomplished and outstanding editors. Tis nobler in the mind!

To my beautiful and intelligent wife, Ann, who tolerates the many hours of my absence.

There is a time and place for us…

Prologue
Tomato

When Maishe Rosstein cut into the cherry tomato, resting on top of his salad that Sunday evening at 8:12 P.M., March 15, 1985, he saw that it bled over the lettuce. It cried out to him in agony.

It yelped as a tomato might yelp, squealing a squeak that resembled a whistle, a whistle, however, that clearly was the cry of a wounded vegetable in pain. The green lettuce was painted in red-seed ooze. What struck Maishe as odd about the incident was that it did not strike him as odd at all. It struck him as odd that he considered it transpiring in the normal course of events; he considered it odd that he felt only slight compassion for the sliced organism, in fact, he remembered reading somewhere that one court of cabalists felt that nothing was inanimate; spirit, essence, the life-force, a certain consciousness existed within rocks, stones, trees, fruits, vegetables, as well as within the higher animals. It was, in most cases, only the angels and the demons that could perceive all realms of existences. Only man, a little lower than the angels, somewhat higher than the demons, in most cases, saw them not. Therefore, Maishe thought, it seemed a curious matter that both the demonic host and the angelic host were jealous of men and women. Plato might have included the concept of the universal life-essence in his attempts to discern the ideal; however, in Maishe's own century, neither Sartre's nor Camus's existentialism encompassed enough.

To these skeptics of the twentieth-century scientific mind, the other entity had to gaze through seeing eyes. The tomato might sense, feel, hurt, but it could not observe. It could be plucked from its mother vine, tossed into vats with others of its suffering kind, the cumulative weight of some crushing and dismembering the unfortunate individuals below, they on top unable to assist through the wails and cries of their suffering, squished, seed-bleeding brothers and sisters, then finally to be cut, maimed, bisected, and churned beneath gnashing white, silver banded mercury-laden grindstones in a gaping black hole, doomed to slither down a mucus-filled tube, what was left out of mastication, to be squirted with acids, absorbed into oblivion, abolished.

Yet, thought Maishe, even as he apologized to the tomato, the truth of it was that the tomato, like all life, ultimately becomes part of the consciousness and essence of some other life-entity. Plato might not have thought that, but Aristotle might have.

Well, after all, Maishe Rosstein thought, *Who is to say that a tomato cannot feel, think, express, hurt?*

"I am sorry," Maishe said, "People have to eat vegetables. It is the nature of things."

"Vegetables are important for your health. I wish you had eaten them when you were a child. You remember, Jayne—I never could get him to eat his vegetables when he was little."

This last was said nether by Maishe nor by the tomato, he had sliced into pain and squeal. It had been said by his eighty-year-old mother. Her hair had long ago thinned and turned gray. Her glasses bespoke the age of horned rims; they were thick; still, she experienced difficulty seeing. Nonetheless, overall, she felt in excellent health. She still enjoyed life with a zest. She still told the near and far world, anyone, who would listen, every detail of Maishe's childhood or any other aspect of his private life that she knew about.

Maishe was thankful his mother remained healthy and full of life. Only last year, not even nine full months ago, she had needed emergency gall bladder surgery. She had recovered faster than a woman half her age might have done. In this regard, Maishe considered himself fortunate. He was unhappy that she told everyone, relatives, friends, strangers, everything. Over the years, however, like the tomato that now sat before him bleeding and screaming, he had become reconciled to his fate.

Maishe had come to dinner with his mother, his Aunt Jesse (everyone had always called her Jayne, though no one knew why), and his 19-year-old daughter, Natalie (everyone called her Natalie; Maishe preferred the name he had given her, Natasha Shalom Hyacinth). They sat at Hasenour's Restaurant, at Barret and Grinstead Drive, in Louisville, Kentucky. Hasenour's was one of the finer restaurants. It took Maishe back a bit when he realized he had attained the facility to understand the consciousness of tomatoes in such a place, not in a cheaper coffee shop.

"Tell me," Maishe said, "Are all tomatoes alive—that is, with speech and thought, or just you?"

There was no answer, and Maishe knew the truth of the matter. The tomato's consciousness had departed. He had gone to tomato heaven. Maishe hoped, for the tomato's sake, that it was a better place than this vale of tears where knives cut one's skin and rendered agony where there had been wonder, and where people we loved dearer than others, ratted every aspect of our private lives.

For some reason, Maishe thought of Poe, Shakespeare, and the Bible, and said directly to his mother, aunt, and daughter,

"Tell me, is there…is there balm in Gilead?"

"Daddy, did you hurt your palms again?" Natasha asked.

"You are so bizarre."

"It's true, Jayne," his mother said. "Her name was Sarah. Sarah Pierce Rosstein. I don't know what to do. He's always scratching or cutting his hands or fingers."

It was true. Maishe could pass his hand over a banister, even a few inches above the wood, and splinters flew through the air, as if the banister hurled darts into the palms of his hand; at a grocery store, he would extrude a bascart from the line of its fellows, and chrome slivers from the cage found their way into the juncture of his finger and palm. Often it seemed to him as though these shards lay in wait for him, Maishe Rosstein, plotting, coiled to spring when his hand and no other's passed over them, and then refused to dislodge despite coaxing of needle and tweezer.

It was the jealous demons, he knew. They were always after him. And now they used innocent wood and metal parts which wanted only to be left alone, he was sure.

"No, Natalie. I'm all right. I think I suddenly have a clearer vision of things now, well, even a tomato has to live and die."

Maishe knew the noise in the restaurant, which was considerable, was only part of the answer. Even his own family ignored or misinterpreted most of what he said. It had been that way since fifth grade. One day, during the teacher's temporary absence, his classmates accused him falsely of talking in class. In actuality, they had been talking while he had been reading a biography of Abraham Lincoln. It had been a fascinating biography. He had liked the character of the book as well as the content of its text. The book had had an orange cover, hard-back but flexible; the print had been deep black, ebony; the pictures had also been deep black, for they were silhouettes. He remembered the silhouettes raising slightly off the page. He liked to run his fingers over this outline.

But it was neither the intelligence of the work nor the aesthetic of its design that followed him; rather, the false accusations and misinterpretations had plagued him and haunted him.

Now it was clear to him at last what he must do. He approached his fiftieth birthday. It was time to see the world.

The dinner continued. *Well, all life is cruel and cannibal,* thought Maishe; still, after all, it would be a gross non-sequitur if he sacrificed his own sentience and survival for that of a tomato.

Even zebras and gazelles sprinted mere beef on the hoof served to lions, tigers, cheetahs, and, it was now revealed by Jane Goodall's brilliant work, occasionally chimpanzees and other apes. In our own woods, American, wolves, coyotes, pumas, cougars, foxes, eagles, falcons, what was left of them, devoured deer, birds, rabbits, squirrels, chipmunks, mice. The most insatiable maw of all was humanity's gullet. Man, woman, predators. All one had to do was gaze at his or her reflection in the mirror to see the truth. Only predators looked straight ahead; only predators seated canine fangs within their rows of teeth. The prey looked to the side and ground only molars. Yes, but man upset the balance of the nature of things.

He misinterpreted the Biblical injunction to take dominion as to take possession, as to dominate, rather than to nurture, to tend, to care for. Maishe gazed about the room. Other patrons dined amidst laughter, looks of sophistication as fake as their eyelashes. At the next table, two flamboyant women discussed their nails. One, a large-boned charismatic woman whom Maishe could not keep his eyes off of, dressed in what seemed a nineteenth-century theatrical costume, admired the plaque fingernails of her companion. Maishe looked at the fingernails. They were not merely long, but broad, and a miniature Chinese painting appeared on each nail.

Through the cacophony of drifting table talk wafting all about him, through her deep-throated laugh, Maishe heard the large woman say, "Why, darling, they are darling. Aren't they, darling?" She said the last to her companion on her other side, laughing again, a healthy, sensuous, deep-breathy laugh.

Maishe could see the deep red-purple of her gums, her teeth fully exposed. This gesture reduced her almost ugly. It clearly showed the features of the predator, however, death ripping flesh once alive, even in the joy and throes of laughter. Still, Maishe continued to be fascinated with her. Suddenly, he imagined himself captured by these two women. Clearly, neither he nor any man would be a match for them.

They preferred perversions, erotic, unspeakable acts of cruelty and kindness upon the bodies of men. In a moment, Maishe realized with astonishment, his own body responded to his fantasy even under the dinner table in Hasenour's. Since he knew himself, a pudgy, fifty-year-old short, bald man had no hope with this amazing creature, he turned again to devour the life forms before him.

******

Only a few days before this dinner, Maishe had met a girl.

He had been crossing Bardstown Road just north of Taylorsville Road. When he visited, he lived in the area with his mother.

He was returning from Kroger Grocery with an item or two. When he heard her laugh he fell in love. It wasn't the laugh so much as it was her situation wherein she laughed.

******

Her car, having failed her, was being towed away. She seemed fetching, and Maishe had said, offhand, as he approached her side of the street, "Not one of your better days?" And she laughed, long and low and loud and somehow fetching. She wore pants, bright, yellow, loose,

She was short, with hair that somehow seemed short yet cascaded in bobs about her shoulders.

"Look, ah, you can say no and no is no, I understand that—well, that is—you'll pardon me, it has been a long time since I, that is, you seem to be having a bit of a hard time.

"I was wondering if you would agree to do me the honor of being my guest at lunch. It seems you could use…"

"I'd love to."

"…a break here, to put it in the vernacular, and—you would?"

He took her to Hasenour's. He sat here contemplating the large wondrous woman of mystery and her companion with the fingernails. It struck him as strange that he might not have been at this restaurant five times in his life, and here he was twice within a month. It struck him now as he found his body responding again that the two dinners had been consumed at this same table.

Her name Marcia but she pronounced it Marsiah. He was taken with her at once. They talked and joked and laughed away the entire lunch. From her heavenly sphere upon the wall, a delicate angel, wrapped in soft cottony cloth, crowned with a diadem of small flashing white lights, watched over them. It seemed a curious matter to him that at the first meal the angel appeared to wink at him with her left eye, and, now, at the second meal, with her right eye.

He spent the afternoon with Marcia that day. Although he was astonished that his body responded as well as it did, he also knew that in today's world, one had to be careful. So it was without entrance that they agreed to entertain one another; throughout the long, lazy afternoon it was clear they had both enjoyed the game of it. Her body, her sweet scent, her short, bobbing hair, and her laugh—except for the amazing woman at the next table, Maishe couldn't get her out of his mind.

The truth of the matter was, it had been his first sexual experience for some time. Soon, far out on the prairie, he would have to return to his wife. He was not looking forward to it. He liked it better here, in his home town, and now that he had found Marcia, he didn't want to live anywhere else. He had explained this to Marcia on the second afternoon of their affair. She now knew he would soon have to leave. She did what she always did when she was upset. She laughed. The dinner ended, it was time to leave the restaurant.

Maishe, his mother, his aunt, his daughter, left. He took a last look at the wall angel with its lights blinking and its right eye winking at him; he cast a last longing glance at the Amazon angel holding court at her table. Yes, he knew it was time to see the world.

******

Maishe and his daughter returned to Omaha, Nebraska, to their home on South 90th Street, one block south of Center Street, a dormer-story yellow house with a large yard for their dog to run around in. The yard continued in back, opening out onto the running track of the local school district's middle school's athletic field. One night thereafter, Maishe's wife blew up at Natasha. She told her daughter to leave home.

The family's dog was an Australian Blue Rider, black and gray, gentle and kind. As the years rolled by, Maishe's wife had gotten tougher, heavier, meaner. As the years rolled by, Maishe began to suspect that he, like the dog, had become calmer, gentler (albeit heavier as well, he was compelled to confess).

Somewhere he had recently read a study that it was like that for most men and women, their aging occurring in this peculiar fashion of dichotomy. He recalled the article indicated it had something to do with testosterone levels, that men's levels decreased, that women's levels increased as they, male and female, proceeded with their incredible journey through life.

Maishe had never been successful in a career or in business. Others, he knew, including, he always reckoned, his wife, saw this as a weakness. In time, Maishe had come even to exaggerate the truth about his jobs, positions, appointments, consultations. He did not produce this misinformation because of any need to appear in a certain light. In truth, Maishe had never understood any of it, the constant scratching, biting, gnashing of teeth for increased material gain. His own needs simple: a warm residence in winter, a cool one in summer; good, fresh food; a hot cup of coffee in the morning and a cold Diet-Rite Cola in the afternoon and evening; spring and autumn walks with his dog in the park; scribbling a few lines on a page of paper, like these, in the morning, puttering through his correspondence and papers in the afternoon and evening; watching one or two favorite television programs; a good movie now and then; comfortable clothes; a comfortable couch»-these were all he needed.

He would have preferred even not to have a car. He dreamed of being able to walk to a location when he would work in the afternoon or evening at a place to make enough money to live and to enjoy the things he enjoyed. It was the tragedy and the blessing of his life that he had married and had fathered a daughter. He had wanted to stay in his own home town. He had been compelled to move, He had wanted a simple life. He stumbled through one complicated.

He wanted to be surrounded by women. Until his academic career began, he had discharged duties surrounded by other men. He had wanted his work to be recognized and admired. He was ignored. His one bright spot had been his daughter. In her perhaps lay some salvation. Now she was gone, sent away from the house by the wife grown heavy and mean-spirited.

Through the night he searched for her. He drove up and down Center Street. He drove along the side numbered streets; 84th, 88th, 90th, 108th, 102nd, 94th. Finally, he checked into a motel. He called her friends. He found her at last at Chancey's. He picked her up. He brought her back to the motel.

In the morning, she agreed it was time to go away to school. That afternoon Maishe Rosstein went to the bank. He cleaned out his accounts. Most of the money he gave to his daughter. The family was breaking up now, he knew, and Natalie would need every penny until she could get a job and assistance.

He advised her to go back to Louisville and move in with her grandma; but she didn't want to leave her friends. Maishe had never had many friends, but he could understand others having them and not wanting to leave them.

He waited until he was sure his wife had left the house for the day. He returned to pack a few things. He called the college to tell them an emergency had come up and he couldn't return for a while. Then, he left. He found it odd that the hardest thing he had to do was pet and tell his dog goodbye.

He hoped his wife would take care of him and not give him away. He thought about taking him, then thought better of it and left. He was sure she would take care of him. She was, after all was said and done, a good woman under a great deal of stress. Well, now there would be more—or less. For a moment, he considered taking the dog. In the end, he left him. It was hard. He knew she would take care of him.

For a while, he entertained joining the army. After all, there was a war on. He passed by the recruiting center. He saw lean, tough men going in and out, or young men and women. That life, for him, was over, and it was that loss which he felt deepest of all. He passed out of town in silence, tears rolling down his cheeks unanswered. For some reason, he drove south on U. S. 75. All he could see in front of him was the bright red blood of the cherry tomato.

1

Cucumber

It was a 1975 Vega two-door wagon hatchback. It was green. If it had been a darker shade, from a distance it would have looked like a cucumber. But it was neon-lime green, the color of those old twin popsicle bars one used to acquire at the corner grocer's thirty, forty years ago, Maishe remembered the black lining around the large plexiglass doors of the freezers. He opened them up, away from him. They were a bit heavy and he had to work at it; then, finally, the spring caught and they stood upright as if saluting; then he had to reach down, way down, into the deep of the freezer. He grabbed the popsicle by the flat wooden sticks inserted into the frozen ice, and pulled up, hoping the angle and purchase tension wouldn't cause the confection to break in the half across the top.

They were double teepees of frozen flavor, united through the center by a flap of themselves, Siamese twins. He liked tearing the thin red, blue, black, and white paper slowly and parts of it always stuck. Parts of the treat always stuck to the paper too, and no matter how much he tried to avoid it his hands were sticky even before he began to lick the bright—lime green ice sickle. He recalled, he could never get all the way through without the two conjoined pieces breaking. But the best was at the end when only a remnant remained on the sticks and he pushed them up and down, letting the texture more than the taste linger.

That was the color of the 1975 Vega two-door wagon that, had it been a darker shade of green might have resembled not a popsicle but a cucumber. As it left Omaha and passed through Bellevue, approaching Offutt Air Force Base, the Vega's odometer read 77,387 miles. It still ran like a top and got 32 miles to the gallon. Most of them, he knew, rusted out after a while, but he hadn't seen too much evidence of that. It was a fear he had, though, that the car would rust out from under him, even while the engine and drive train seemed they could go on forever. All his cars did that. Maishe was sorry he had never had a car get more than 80 or 90,000 miles.

He felt the usual twinge when he passed Offutt's gates. Even 500 yards in off the highway, he could see the security guard wave the officers' cars in with a smart salute. Over 20 years ago, Maishe had been an officer in the Air Force.

He had always kicked himself for not making the service his career. Maishe had always been confused and easily manipulated. He had known, now for some years, he had a personality disorder.

The condition, he grew to realize, had improved a great deal as he got older; but by then it was too late. At 45 or 50 years of age, one could not re-join the Air Force nor join the police force of a town. Justice and truth had always been important to him but his strong neurosis had allowed his life to be a lie, up to now.

Now his life was over and it was beginning. He had left. As usual, he felt bad and he felt good. But however he felt, he felt like going on. He didn't know where he was going.

He didn't care. He drove, south. Soon the highway, already divided since the air force base, opened into a largely barren expanse, allowing a wide vista. In the distance, Maishe saw a huge plane, a 747 dancing a slow ballet in the air, languidly describing its final approach for landing, as if a piece of the sky had fallen and was floating down along easy drifting currents. It was the National Airborne Command Post, he knew, and it always floated in for a landing, probably to protect its complex and delicate electronic systems.

Soon the long stretch of highway, interrupted by a few hints of civilization, an old fishing lodge hotel, a beach along a small lake, crossed the Platte River, and the highway skirted around Plattsmouth. The Platte was an amazing river, always changing yet never seeming to move. Soon Plattsmouth fell behind him and he rolled on through farmland, and recreational lakes, a dark curving two-lane, black ribbon bordered by brown soil, farmer's land, Nebraskaland, heartland, Midwest land, soil that bore wheat and corn. Usually, as it was today, it was brown and tilled and lay there against the road, a great Midwestern potential answer to all the hunger in the world. Once great species of six and eight-foot prairie grass had stood there, a waving phalanx of infinite plant variety, from coltsfoot to thistle, had undulated from the confluence of Missouri and the Platte, all the way to the foot of the Rocky Mountains, a great sea of grass and weed and life.

Now it was agricultural soil, to be tilled and cleared, and planted with seed to be teeming millions of one species. Maishe, for a moment, cried at the great loss of the variety of grasses and the animal life the fauna had hidden and sustained.

******

He thought about turning off to Lincoln. He thought better of it. He continued south toward Nebraska City. In time, the rich soil gave way to a few apple orchards, a little bit of woods that reminded him of a hint of the great forests of Kentucky. The land had given way to hills and dales as well. Again, for a moment, Maishe entertained turning left, traveling east, returning to the south, to home. After all, for some years now he had desired to return to his home town.

Then, on a brief flat expanse, at the top of a large rolling hill, he saw at a distance, down in the valley of the hill, a girl by the side of the road. She had a canvas Israeli paratrooper pack on the road by her side.

She was slim, yet something about her suggested the strength and power of the athlete. She had long gray-tinged blond-brown hair, as though she had aged before her time yet refused to give away the gladness of youth. At the distance he drove by her she appeared like a vision, clearly a beauty.

Ordinarily, Maishe was a cautious man. After all, there might be an accomplice hiding in the gully beyond her, a heavy man with thick hairy arms and a knife, ready to pounce, slit his throat, and the two of them, the couple, like Bonnie and Clyde, would take his few possessions and his

1975 lime-green Vega that had 77,423 miles on it, which, had it been a few shades darker, might have looked like a cucumber.

He stopped, down the road, so she had to run a distance. He liked watching her run to him, her image dashing across his rearview mirror, a track athlete on a near-empty stretch of black-ribbon farm and orchard country in south-east Nebraska. The pack slumped over her shoulder, bumped against her backside.

She slowed to a cantor, then a walk. He continued scanning the mirror to ensure the evil accomplice did not lurk behind. She slid alongside the car. For an instant, he considered pulling away and leaving her, sort of a perverse punishment to all women who treated him, his daughter, and other men and women wrong.

He reached over. He pulled down the window. She placed her face through the window. For a moment, he thought it was the change in light to shadow, that the shadows cast weird streaks. Then he saw the truth of the matter. Her beauty was tainted, violated, bespeckled, bespattered. Skin tones in a variety of hue and texture, rolled, creased, and crisscrossed astride the girl's near-perfect bone structure, as if someone had melted down the substance, then frozen it as it had reformed in a pattern of lines, creases, folds, circles, grooves, gullies, channels.

Through this mask shined, glistened, glittered two of the most crystal-clear gray-green eyes he had ever seen, jewels, jade, gems, faceted, shining.

"Hi."

"Hi."

"I'm Krystal. You know, like glass. Krystal."

"I'm Maishe."

"Mayess?"

"You can call me Morris, if you like, for a while, anyway,"

"I like Ma-May…"

"…Maishe, like face, only with an sh-fash."

"Yeah. Maishe. I like that better."

"Krystal's pretty."

"Thanks."

"Well…"

"I want to go to Hollywood. I want to be an actress. I know I can't star. My face and all, But they have character parts, they call them, you know. Which way are you going? If you take me down to Highway 2, I can hitch out west."

"Hop in. We'll turn right at Highway 2 and head west. For my part, we'll keep on going. Maybe, I'll drive clear to the ocean, wouldn't that be something?"

"All right."

Krystal, the girl who appeared beautiful at a distance and disfigured up close, got into the bright lime-green Vega, and it headed on toward Nebraska City and the Highway 2 intersection.

"This here's a peculiar green color for a car, ain't it?"

"Isn't it?" Maishe said, despite himself, and smiled.

At least he knew where he was going, more or less.

******

Off the 75 bypass, west of Nebraska City, at the Highway 2 intersection, he turned the Vega west. He drove for an hour through more farmland. Occasionally, towns and villages sprang up to his right side and to his left side, and he was strangely reminded of the passages in Deuteronomy where Moses exhorts his followers to choose the way that is the right way.

Maishe knew he was no longer consciously choosing but reacting. It didn't matter. As Chekhov says through the doctor at the end of *Three Sisters*, "Nothing really matters." What was life, anyway, but a journey, a travel, a sojourn, a vale of tears that led to another journey on a different plane of existence somewhere else? He had been false to his journey all his life; now he was attempting to…

"I'm hungry," Krystal said. "I'm hungry and I have to go to the bathroom. And you haven't said three words to me."

"I'm sorry, Krystal," Maishe said, "I was distracted. I was in a reverie."

"What?"

"I was thinking about something."

"What's wrong? Don't you like me? I know I'm not—I mean, my face and all—"

"No—don't be silly. Of course not. Actually, I happen to think you're very good looking."

"Really?"

"Yes. We'll be in Lincoln in a few minutes. We'll stop there. We'll talk while we eat something. We'll find a place. I'd better get some gasoline too."

She looked out the window. For a moment she sat, quiet. From time to time he glanced over. He enjoyed the images of her hand, her neck, the side of her creased jawline, with an almost grayish patch of skin. A few houses, suburbs of the city appeared to his right side and to his left side. He began to look for a place to stop. A series of commercial strips and shopping centers drew up ahead.

"The thing of it is," Maishe said, "I left my wife and my home today. I'm fifty years old. I could be your father or even your—I hope you don't mind. That is to say."

He saw she was looking at him. "It's OK by me," she said, "I think you're cute. I'm sorry about your wife, though. You won't hurt me or beat me or nothing, will you?"

"Or anything. No—never."

"Teach me to talk right. Will you do that? Will you teach me to talk right and stuff? Teach me things, right ways of doing things, will you?"

"Here's a place," Maishe said.

He pulled the Vega into the parking lot of a diner. The odometer now read 77, 501 miles.

Maishe noticed it when he turned off the key. Krystal and he got out of the car, locked it, and walked together into the diner. The girl looked at him almost the entire way, as if she was seeing something, hope perhaps, for the first time.

2

Radish

It sat on his bed of lettuce, one lonely radish, cut in a flowing pattern, as a fountain might spew forth water, seven tips cut away from the top of the radish, the side opposite from where it had been separated from its leaf. Maishe picked the radish up. He twirled it in his fingers. He looked at its underside. He saw the circle of darkness where once the radish had attached itself whole to its leafy stem that had seen the sun and felt the rain and ensured the nutrition to feed the round red, fat, miracle root, bursting with nutrition.

Now it had been cut twice. It had been ripped, stem from the root, and its top had been peeled back to give a certain visual appeal to travelers and locals who entered this diner on the eastern outskirts of Lincoln, Nebraska, to get a bite to eat.

"And are you going to give me more pain, before you devour me?"

Maishe looked around, startled. Suddenly he realized that, again, like the tomato before it, the radish spoke to him.

"Perhaps, you know the tomato," Maishe said, "I discussed the inevitable construct of this reality with the tomato. Surely you must know the same truth. All things exist only to be consumed by other things, in their time. Your time has come now. My time will come later. In this ultimate truth, we are connected. And, in turn, that ultimate truth connects us with some life form in the past and with one in the future. Something that died gave birth to you. When I die, something in the future will consume my nutrients and life. And so it goes. Time comes to all and life goes on in this fashion of death. The truth is, nothing can live without something else giving up its life. This is the existential reality under which we are all blessed and cursed."

"I never thought of it that way," the radish said, "still it's a terrible thing to be champed up while still here and needing, wanting, desperately desiring a few more minutes, even a few more seconds. At least, you'll be long gone. You will not have to linger in torment."

"I guess, that's so," Maishe said. "Actually, I guess that's one of the differences between vegetables and animals. But, the ultimate truth is, it doesn't matter. As the doctor in *Three Sisters* says, 'Nothing really matters.'"

"Oh my, I feel so much better," the radish said.

"I'll tell you what," Maishe said.

He saw Krystal at a distance. She was walking from the bathroom to their table.

He was struck again by her beauty at a distance. He noticed people passing her close gave her that strange second look he was sure he had given her. He wondered if she ever got used to those second looks, then the avoidance of looking, the same second look and avoidance of looking he imagined people in wheelchairs or with severe palsy or with pronounced speech defects had to inure themselves against if they could ever become used to it all.

"I'll give you to be eaten by a beautiful woman."

"I feel so much better," the radish said. "After all, teeth are teeth, a tongue is a tongue, a mucous filled throat is a mucous filled throat, and a gullet is a gullet, with its acids and enzymes and other devouring, burning, destroying substances."

"Forgive me, radish, but a beautiful woman with scars also has to live,"

"I'm back," Krystal said.

"I saved this radish for you," Maishe said.

"Thanks," Krystal said. "I love radishes. I never got none growing up. Not many, anyways."

"I never got any," Maishe said. "And it's anyway, not anyways."

"I never got n…anyway… I never got any, anyways," Krystal said and smiled a smile with the shimmering deep blue eyes that knocked his socks off.

Maishe started to say something. Instead, he smiled back.

Krystal ate the radish, whole, her lips curled around the red part for a while. Maishe realized that for an instant he had not noticed her mask of creases.

******

A rough, hoarse sound invaded their privacy; by degrees, the hacking waxed to an intolerable fit; increasingly Maishe grew aware of a man at a nearby table. As their meals progressed, the cough worsened. It emerged, along with their dessert, a great snorting, whooping, gasping. But that occurred toward the end of their dessert. During their salad, Maishe told her his story.

An old-style jukebox selected remnants of records. Music pervaded the restaurant, whispering tunes in the filtering fringes of the air. The restaurant was glass-enclosed on all three sides. Its tabletops were plastic. Metal napkin holders allowed patrons to pull out a napkin. Usually, more than one napkin pulled out, the fellow stuck to the one being yanked from the metal container. Occasionally, the container split open at the top, where it was filled, and an entire pad of napkins spilled out. Maishe tried to push the pile of napkins back into the container. The napkins refused to return. It was as if, once freed, they refused to be contained again.

Maishe wondered if they too were not the inanimate objects they seemed. After all, like the tomato and the radish, they were developed from organic materials. True, the analogy could not quite hold together. After all, the tomato and the radish were plucked whole, complete, and manipulated in the same form.

The paper in the metal holders had been taken from trees, a great life form, but had been abused terribly, bleached properly, and left out to dry. It was a curious matter. It was a strange matter.

Maishe wondered if perhaps nothing truly was inanimate, if all objects held some essence of life left, some indefinable quality that they maintained, or that entered them without ceremony once they were created. If that were so, Maishe realized, then his car, the Vega, that, with a different shade of hue, might resemble a cucumber, could also fall into what was evolving into an expanded category.

He looked out the window. He observed the car. It sat on the asphalt lot (did even mixed surfaces such as asphalt or concrete fall into this emergent mold; what of paint, such as the yellow parking sections?) seemingly inanimate, but now…Maishe began to suspect more. It seemed to him that the Vega grinned at him, perhaps knowingly.

Glint-beams and reflections of rays bounced from chrome, glass, metal off a sun low in the western sky. The light hurt his eyes. The glares rebounded here and there, into the distance, from the parking lot, out to where traffic moved along the street, a shifting, jostling mass of moving, glaring metal, each metallic unit casting its sheen, each ferrying its passengers to their destination. Maishe knew his destination now washed in the great ocean at the end of the land of that setting sun.

As he turned back to say something sweet and charming to the girl, he found himself looking down suddenly at the back of a man's head. The hair was gray, sprinkled around a large bald spot. Red ooze, much like the tomato's spurts, turned the white napkins toward scarlet. The hair spread about, like the radish had been fluted like a floret, surrounding the bald pate, in a sparse, floral arrangement, not like a bouquet, but like one, old wilted rose. The metal container also lay flattened beneath the head, and the red ooze emanating out from the under the head was not the lymph flow of tomatoes nor of radishes.

It was interesting to Maishe that he looked up and saw the girl's eyes open wide, and her mouth, a large crevasse like a funnel of crevices, dilated, wide, almost looking like a woman's vaginal fold, also a flower, also petals, before he heard the scream shudder from deep within her.

"Oh, God, Maishe, he's…he's dead. He coughed and then he keeled over. He's dead."

Maishe always knew what to do in emergencies, in fact, these rare and few times were the only times that he knew what he was doing with his life.

"Krystal, Calm down. Look into my eyes."

"Oh, God. Oh God, Maishe."

"I said look into my eyes. Look! I'm going to do everything that needs to be done here. Just do what I say. Calm down. Now! Good. Now go to the phone. It's over there. Dial 911. Tell them what's going on. Go…and stay calm."

People craned their necks. They gaped at the accident.

Some began to take hesitant steps toward his table. A few crowded around. Maishe heard the man gurgle. He heard the man wheeze. He noticed his hands were around his throat, not around his stomach or chest.

Maishe stood up behind the man, put his arms about him, felt for his rib cage, placed his thumbs into the sternum, just below where it ended and pulled back and up hard. The man grunted. Maishe repeated the procedure. Something flew out from the man's throat, bounced across the table, and slid out of sight.

Maishe leaned the man back. He saw blood oozing down from his nose. He loosened the man's tie.

After a few moments, the man gasped, "You…you saved my life."

"Well, I am sure someone would have…"

"No. No, it was you. Here, take these. I can't make it tonight. Not now."

The man pushed an envelope into Maishe's hand. He got up. He dashed out. He got into his car. He drove away.

Maishe hollered at him to wait until emergency services arrived. It was no use. The man was gone.

Maishe turned the envelope over in his hand. It was brown, old, wrinkled, creased. *Part of it looked like Krystal's face,* Maishe thought. Immediately he felt ashamed for the thought. After all, he found himself captivated by the girl.

Captivated? It was far worse. He admitted, at last, he was falling in love, like a schoolboy, at his age. It was ridiculous. He would be besotted. He would lose everything, including the world to come. He suddenly realized she stood next to him.

"Hey," she said.

"Hey," Maishe said.

They smiled.

"Where's the…?"

"He left," Maishe said. "It's all very strange. One moment he's on the table, the next moment he's out the door."

Maishe thought he heard the first distant sound of the wailing siren.

"They won't have anyone to tend to. It's all very strange."

There was no longer any doubt. The siren wailed in the distance.

"You did very well."

"You were wonderful. You were magnificent," Krystal said.

He couldn't be sure. After all, what man or woman could ever be completely sure of the other in the relationship? Maishe Rosstein thought he saw admiration and hero-worship in the girl's brilliant, glistening eyes. For an instant, it seemed to him, he saw her without the scars, the scratches, the crevices, and patch-quilt pattern of flesh glued upon flesh as if it had once melted and condensed back into the wrong pattern; he saw her as she was meant to be, clear, complete, whole, and even more beautiful than he had imagined. Then, as it must have happened at the time, the patterns returned.

The puzzle of skin—pieces assembled into place. But he thought he might have seen love there. At my age, he thought. *She could be my daughter,* he thought. Still, he was glad to find, that, for a moment, at least, he felt like he was twenty-five again. Then he knew that next to hope, love was the greatest feeling, for with it one felt young.

"You know, Krystal, hope is the most powerful force in the universe but love is wonderful at any age. God, I can't believe I told you that."

"You were magnificent," Krystal said.

Suddenly, she found herself a lead singer for a chorus of well-wishers, customers, cooks, cashiers, waitresses, all telling him what a superb job he had done. *It's funny,* Maishe thought. Young or old, when you take the road your life can change. An old Yiddish proverb came to mind. If you live long enough, your life will change; sometimes it will change for the better; sometimes it will change for the worse; but, rest assured and take comfort—it will change.

"What is that?" Krystal said. She pointed to the brown, wrinkled envelope he held in his hand. Maishe was astonished to find he had forgotten about it.

The sirens approached closer now. Soon he knew they would be in the parking lot. The doors would slam. At once, competent, efficient, expectant men and women in uniform would take charge in the restaurant.

"It's a…he gave it to me. He shoved it in my hands as he ran out."

"Let me see," Krystal said. And she gently took it. It seemed odd to him that he noticed for the first time she had no scars on her hands.

She opened the envelope. It crinkled in sound more than he thought the old envelope would. "It's tickets of some sort. What is it?"

"Let me see." The rescue vehicle was in the lot. A man and a woman in uniform were getting out. "These are tickets for a play."

People from the restaurant, the waitress at the lead, he noticed, were trying to explain the situation to the rescue workers before they accumulated their equipment. "Why, they're for tonight. They're at the university playhouse. *Three Sisters*. It's a play by Anton Chekhov."

"Who?"

"Chekhov. He was a late nineteenth, early twentieth-century playwright who did much to—yeah, well, I'll explain later. For now, do you want to go?"

She crinkled her nose. Her eyes glistened. "You betcha," she said. "Can we? Will you take me? Can I walk to the theater, it is a playacting theater, ain…isn't it? Can I walk to the playacting theater holding onto your arm, like a sophisticated lady-like, can we…"

"Krystal. Yes to all inquiries."

She crinkled her nose. She smiled. Her eyes glistened in depth all the way back to creation and home again. *God, Maishe thought. It's true. I am in love again.* And he heard the host of angels by the Right Leg of the Footstool. They didn't sing. They laughed.

******

Although a large arts center and operatic size theater recently constructed stood like mocking sentinels across the street from the theater department, the department continued to stage its productions in the theater housed within its own building, Until the new art center had been built, this theater seemed large, expansive. *A 400-seater, maybe,* Maishe thought, *well, probably closer to 350. Continental style seating, it must have seemed modern, contemporary at the time it was built, probably in the 1950s.* Today it simply looked serviceable, used. It had settled into being something comfortable, an old easy chair of a theater where one saw plays, productions probably, for the most part of a semi-professional quality. After all, at a university, a department this size,

Maishe had little doubt that graduate students, professionally trained actors, really, won nearly all the plum, coveted roles. Maishe wondered about the undergraduate students. Probably working crew—stagehands, grips, light crew, slave laborers to stand in awe backstage, beyond the teasers, tormentors, batons, in the wings, knowing they have this raw talent, watching the technique trained with awe and with envy proceed through their mentors' rehearsed paces, the lights of the ellipsoidals, fresnels, strips, floods, sparkling in the deep-set reflections of their eyes.

Well, Even in Greece, as actors in great three-dimensional helmet-masks tromped in huge costumes within gigantic stadium theaters under the blazing sun of daylight, spouting words and language as magnificent as any written since, words of Sophocles and Euripides, wherein men and women tempted the fates and the anger of the gods themselves yet endeavored to gain a spark of the divine themselves—even within this early theater of theaters, there had to have been would-be and wannabe actors in the wings gazing dreamily out onto the chorus circle at the skine, starry-eyed and stage-struck. Some things never change.

Only technology changes. Men and women stay the same. *What curious creatures we are,* Maishe thought. We exist the lowest of slime-scum wretchedness, while a highly developed mind can write Olympian language for Oedipus or Medea and some other highly formed personalities can interpret them on a raised platform to other highly developed personages to ponder. What a rogue and peasant slave, and what a thing of wonder. Jeckell and Hyde. Physician and monster.

"Whatcha thinkin' about?"

It took him a moment to realize Krystal addressed him. "What?"

He felt his face flush. He realized that for an instant he had forgotten about Krystal and considered, for the first time since he left, his wife. What was she doing now? What was she thinking? She must be shocked. After all, she probably never considered that he would leave. The old refrain of the Glen Campbell song returned to him. "By the Time I Get to Phoenix…" He didn't hear it played much anymore. There was a time when almost any time you turn on the radio you heard a Glen Campbell song. Now there was only talk on the radio. As if being a radio announcer made anyone an expert on anything—yet there they were, spouting their own idiotic spews of garbage and allowing their callers to spout emotional claptrap as if it were gospel when it was only gossip.

Maishe liked Glen Campbell. He liked the way he sang. He liked him in that movie with John Wayne and Kim Darby where Wayne won his academy award—*True Grit*, a fine piece of work. Years ago, Maishe had attended the premiere of *True Grit* in Little Rock, Arkansas. In those years he lived in Little Rock because he was an officer in the air force, and he was stationed at Little Rock Air Force Base. The movie premiered in Little Rock because the man who wrote the book lived there and the setting was Arkansas. The amazing thing was, Maishe had lived next door to the man, to the writer. They had lived side by side in apartment cubicles on Eucalyptus Street. The complex had a coke-bottle shaped swimming pool in the center of the L-shaped legs of apartment cubicles. The complex overlooked the Arkansas River.

Maishe had a secret spot, a cove in a bend of the river that he went to think and write a little himself. One day, he went down to his cove and saw discarded beer bottles there. He left and never returned. Maishe was young and a military man. He came and went to the base to work at his job, wrote a little, dreamed a lot, and heard the writer's typewriter tapping half the day. Then the premiere of the movie was in Little Rock and, although he only saw the writer occasionally on the hall-balcony leading to their rooms, the man, the writer of the book from which the movie was made, invited him.

He was disappointed that neither Wayne nor Darby showed up; but Glen Campbell did, and, although he didn't meet him, he saw him close enough. Campbell was from Arkansas, and for him, it was a homecoming. The governor proclaimed it Glen Campbell Day. The governor had not been born in Arkansas. The governor had been born in New England (Maishe thought it was New York) and he was a member of the Rockefeller family.

"Maishe?"

"Hmm?"

"Whatcha thinkin' about?"

"Hmm? Oh, nothing, really. Just thinking about the theater, I guess. And it's 'What are you,' not 'Whatcha,' and 'thinking,' not 'thinkin.'"

"Whatch what whatch ar what are you, what are you thinkin' thinking think-ing, th-thinking."

Maishe knew he was captured, hopelessly hooked. He leaned over to catch her scent. There was the smell of burned and seminal flesh, no doubt—a sickly-sweet indefinable smell, a smell we're not meant to smell and so our brain doesn't quite know how to interpret it; yet there was also the strong scent of the young, healthy female, a woman-heaven scent, from her hair, the nape of her neck, just under her arms, between her breasts, just inside her thigh, and, of course, from that wonderful moist honey-heaven of womanhood—the most wonderful organ, tissue in all the human body.

"Right. 'What are you thinking?' Say it five times, in a row, correct."

The girl obeyed him dutifully, without hesitation. It was a wonderful new feeling for him, to wield power over a hopeful spirit, to have the one you love, obey your command. It was not the first time he considered it, but Maishe found himself wondering if any woman had furtively pretended to be a man, so she could be an actor in the ancient Greek or Hellenistic theaters. He'd laid down his money that there was one or two. After all, the human spirit is such that…

"How do you pronounce his name again?"

It would be a wonderful research project for a graduate student or a faculty member, for that matter; in fact, it could be a career-maker, an article or even a book…

"Maishe?"

"Hmm? Oh, ah, Chekhov Tchekhov—like the crewman on Star Trek, the original one. Same pronunciation," Maishe said.

He liked Star Trek, the first and the new. He considered himself a Trekkie.

"And these others—how can anyone say them?"

"Don't worry about it. Remember their first names—Olga, Masha, Irina. Olga is the oldest. Masha is a beautiful one. Irina is the youngest. When the play opens, it is Irina's birthday. Later she thinks days like that, days spent away from Moscow, days spent away from the city lights, days spent away from one's home, are not always so gay."

"Gay?"

"Not queer. Joyful. Happy. Olga has the first speech. It's important to listen carefully to everything she says. It's the most important exposition."

"What's that?"

"Exposition. To tell us what happened before. To bring us up to date. If you listen carefully to Olga's opening speech, the rest of the play will make more sense for you. And then you'll want to follow it." It occurred to Maishe he had to take her at some point to see, well, rent the video he supposed, Woody *Allen's Hannah and Her Sisters* and ask her for a comparative analysis. The house lights dimmed to half.

For a moment, Maishe caught a brief glimpse of the people behind him, three couples, leaning a bit toward his row; it was clear they had been listening to his own critical analysis and theatrical appreciation advice. He felt strange and he felt good. Krystal noticed them too.

"Maishe, everyone's listening to what you have to say about the play."

"Yes, well, we're starting now. We'll see."

"Here we go," Krystal said. And from somewhere deep in her purse, she took out some glasses he had not yet seen and put them across the bridge of the nose that crinkled cute sometimes. She squinted her eyes; then, as the house went to dark and the stage lights came up, her eyes relaxed and she settled back and leaned forward at the same time, captivated by the color, swish, and swirl of Chekhov's glorious ensemble on stage. The cloister of three women downstage, the gaggle of three men laughing at the dining table upstage, the birch trees, suggestions of them, beyond.

It was so Chekhovian and gave a hint of a decent production of one of the truly great works of art in the world.

******

They were good actors who had received a competent direction. Maishe was not disappointed, He especially liked the actress portraying Masha. She struck the right pose of dissolute, languid, bored beauty, another in Chekhov's endless progression of specimens with vivid, blazing potential, existing in boring marriages, lost career opportunities, affairs of flesh to alleviate ennui. There was some sense of Chekhov's intent, Maishe saw. However, as usual, the humor the playwright inevitably borrowed from his skits and one-acts was missing. The production almost collapsed from this common trap, this pitfall companies doing Chekhov generally tripped into.

Finally, the report of the shot rang out, the band played, and the women, now, in effect, locked out of their own house, lamented at the end as they did at the opening, yet endured. Dreary their lives may be, but their greatness lies in their courage to go on, to hope. Hope, Maishe knew well, was the most powerful force in the universe. He had often considered that there lay the greatness of Chekhov. Like any competent physician, the good doctor evaluated completely, diagnosed accurately, prescribed appropriate treatment, and stimulated a measure of hope.

Yes, he had liked Jenny Vannel Williams, the actress who portrayed Masha. She reminded him of another actress he had known years before, an actress who had dazzled him with her beauty, her charm, her talent, her interpretation of the part. Her name was Charlotte, but everyone called her Charlie and he had been her stage manager. He had fallen in love then too, for she was, he knew, finding the truth that Chekhov had intended to be found in the part.

In fact, Charlie had become Masha. Maishe knew that had he been alive and around to see her, Stanislavsky himself would have been pleased with Charlie's interpretation. He considered taking Krystal backstage to meet Jenny, then thought better of it. The lights faded on Olga's final words of hope, and even before they returned full, the audience was applauding. Her eyes were full of the lights of the stage, the color of the costumes, the language of genius.

"It…it was wonderful. Wonderful. I didn't much like that woman who took over their house, though, she was mean, I think. But I loved the sisters. And the Baron. He was so nice. I hated it when he killed himself. But I know why he had to. It was his honor at stake, wasn't that it?"

"Yes, Krystal."

"Yea, I knew it. I knew--oh wow, thanks ever so much for bringin'—for bringing me. You knew I'd like it, didn't you? You knew?"

"I thought you might."

"Maishe?"

"Yes?"

"You'll take me to a motel tonight won't you?"

"Yes, Krystal. We'll stop in Grand Island. It's about two hours away. Maybe not that much."

"You…you don't think I'm ugly, do you? I mean, my scars and…"

He put his hand on her mouth. Then, totally infatuated with her and with the production and with high art, himself, besotted, he realized he kissed her, a long, delicious, sweet smooch. It felt so good, so marvelous, he wondered why he had let himself go so long without one. There had been Marcia, of course, but this, with Krystal, was different.

"Oh, here in the theater and all. It was wonderful."

"Oh, Krystal. You are wonderful."

"Maishe?"

"Yes."

"I can do you some good things with the scars on my body, you know."

They were the last ones out. They didn't see the house manager turn out all the lights, as they exited into the night.

3

Celery and Coffee

At night, dancing west on Interstate 80, the long, green line of the front hood of the Vega looked not like a cucumber but a stalk of celery, Maishe thought. The straight lines, the long lines into the florets of the headlamps seeking the road in front reminded him more of the strange vegetable that provided a remarkable addition to chicken soup or roast. It also carried a unique flavor when matched with peanut butter.

Maishe liked the way the peanut butter sometimes lay perfectly in the contours of the well of the crisp sliced celery stalk. The taste was perfect, reminding him of the concept of mutualism in biology. It wasn't like symbiosis, exactly; there was a difference, although he allowed it was difficult to fathom the distinction. In both cases, both species more or less depended for survival or nutriment upon the other and so in return; but in symbiosis, it seemed more immediate and long-term, almost constant. There were those birds that followed whales and ate the barnacles off their backs: The birds received their daily food supply; the whales got a clean, itch-free back.

Maishe had wondered how the birds got water. Did they have a means of filtering salt? For that matter, how did whales and dolphins get the water they needed? Did they have some sort of salt filtration system, a biologic saline-separation device?

Mutualism, on the other hand, seemed more random, or when one species helped another to survive, except once their contact was over, the two species separated until the next time. Bees and flowers for example: The bee visited the flowers, received nectar and pollen—then, in return, upon visiting another plant, ensured the entire species' survival through cross-pollination.

Still, it was difficult to distinguish. Dogs and humans, he thought, were probably symbiotic. The dog had ensured its survival by being protected and cared for; the human, in turn, received undying, unconditional love and loyalty…

"Whatcha, what, what are you thinkin' thinking, what are you thinking about?"

"Beauty. Like yours—and the beauty of the night, the beauty of the road—and nature."

"God, I love to hear you talk."

"Someday, maybe you'll tell me why you were on the road."

"Someday, maybe."

"Yes."

"Maishe."

"Yes."

"Will you order me about, tie my hands behind my back, make me do things, things wonderful and things bad?"

It was not the first time in the past couple of days that Maishe Rosstein had felt stirrings within him as though he were twenty or thirty years old. In fact, Maishe had been curious to read in magazines, the kind usually found in doctor's offices, that men slowed down sexually after forty-five. He found himself getting ever more confident. It seemed to him often that all he could think about were women and how he might approach them.

Sometimes, he wanted a woman three and four times a day. Could the magazines, trusted journals all, have all been in error? Or was he an aberration? Or maybe he had saved it all up? Unlike most young men, he had not been successful with women.

He always been afraid of impotence, or, more accurately, of an inability to maintain an erection for an extended period of time, Now, the older he got, it seemed he was attaining a degree of sexuality most men his age only wished for. He no longer was concerned about a possible blood flow problem--although he knew if he didn't control his weight, there was always a chance he would get diabetes. He did feel so tired most of the time.

"Maishe."

"Yes, Krystal."

"What did you mean, about nature?"

"Move a little closer."

She scooted over a bit. He put his hand on her knee.

He began to work up her thighs toward her womanhood. It was not so gentle, through the thickness and harsh smoothness of her jeans, but there was the whole night in front of them. She leaned back and sighed. He told her of love and symbiotic and mutualistic relationships. She would not get it all, he knew, but he didn't get it all either. Ultimately, he knew, like everything else, it was a great mystery, like a woman, full of wonder. But now, at last, he had a little time.

He drove on, through the night, occasionally scattered lights sprinkled through a few small prairie towns and houses glistened and twinkled in the distance, like stars too far away for us to know, glimmering through the cool night.

******

The motel at Grand Island was directly off the freeway exit. Actually, it seemed to him there was a motel at each of the four corners of the interchange, although one appeared to be a large truck stop. Rural America had become interlaced with these cross-continental ribbons of concrete slicing through fields, meadows, farmland, prairie just on the outskirts of large and medium-sized towns.

Maishe had pulled in to the first one, just as he exited. It had been a long day and a busy night, and he was tired and hungry and, albeit nervous to determine if he could entertain a twenty-year-old woman, he was also looking forward to seeing the design of the scars on her body. He knew she was disfigured, that was all too clear; yet he also knew there was much smooth, soft, supple, responding female flesh. Even in the car, she had moaned something as he sought her womanhood, about the scar above her vulva (she had used the word, cunt, which he also found exciting).

In the morning, he left her sleeping. He was amazed again how at times the scars and mottled-burn-frozen patterns on her face, and, now, on the body he knew, seemed to dissolve into an innocence, a design of the person meant to be. when she slept, filled no doubt with dreams of smooth and righteous flesh covering her, when she ate a certain food or treat she liked, or in the deep twilight of a motel room, wither her body seated astride him, her form and lust and love only beautiful, gorgeous, her breasts swaying above him as he entered her mystery, he knew he had been right. He had astonished both of them. In fact, after a while, he began to be concerned that he might not return to flaccidity again. It was a curious worry for a man, but he knew there was a condition like that and it was in fact considered an emergency. The woman, he noticed, hadn't seemed concerned, simply astonished and happy.

"God, Maishe. Oh God, it's wonderful. I never knew anyone could…"

It was true. He felt he could go on forever and even worried about it and it allowed him to be considerate of her needs. And then, throughout the night, he felt so again himself by responding to her again and again. *Well,* Maishe thought, *now in the cool morning air, it helps to be a late bloomer, if you live long enough.*

Whenever he traveled, it surprised Maishe that the angle of the freeway seemed different somehow in the morning, askew from what he had imagined it to be or recalled it being the night before, when he drove in, stupefied from road exhaustion.

Maishe liked to rise what was considered late in a society founded upon work ethic, about 8:00 or 8:30, drink a cup of decaffeinated coffee, work a little on contests, a hobby of his, putter about on some other things, scribble a few words on five or seven pages, then read, lull, or doze back in bed.

In fact, it suddenly occurred to him that they were in no hurry nor on any schedule. They could see a few sights, the historical area, perhaps, before they continued west to whatever awaited them. Then he smiled, for he realized again, like a couple of young marrieds or lovers, they wouldn't be leaving today for quite another very good reason.

Trucks and cars hummed by, whining and whooshing on the freeway's ribbon of concrete, travelers on the highway of pleasure and business, the infrastructure of our society. It occurred to him that he no longer felt many of the aches and pains that had so plagued him for years. He walked to the coffee shop to start the morning. He might start writing again, but always the need to bring justice to a place where injustice reigned seized him. *Well, he probably had gotten too old for that dream*, he thought.

The thought occurred to him that in the harsh glare of reality's daylight, her face and body might prove ugly; but he thought of her last night. When her eyes glistened and sparkled, and her breasts waved above him like round, soft, spherical golden treasure globes, he caught a glimpse of glory and the divine, and he thought her the most gorgeous woman on earth.

******

Often, he liked to read the morning paper when he traveled and took a cup of coffee. There wasn't much to hold his interest this day. He found he could think only of the woman waiting for him in the room down the way. He could still smell her femaleness, a deep womanly scent, with her, oddly textured by an ever so slight sickly-sweet charred flesh odor, almost like the scent of outdoor cooking just captured below consciousness two blocks away of a summer's eve. Maishe recalled when he and his daughter had stolen outdoors of a clapboard house he had rented for his family. She was seven or eight, then, and they liked to sit together on the porch while their mother and wife busied herself with the dinner dishes.

His wife had been more domestic in those days, before that turn-about time when she took charge of everything, even him, and he had changed, lost so much of spirit and joy and the miracle through which he saw himself. Tonight would be a summer's eve like that, he felt sure. He wondered if Krystal would like to take iced tea on the veranda or patio—if they could find a veranda or patio—the way Natasha liked to in those days. She still did.

That's funny, Maishe thought. *Natasha and Krystal are about the same age and here I am, one's father and the other's lover. If they meet, would they like each other?* He rather thought they would. If Natasha had a lover his age, how would he feel? Not so bad, he realized. The gentleman would, after all, be more considerate of her than boys her own age.

Maishe Rosstein had wanted to run away west for a long time, but he had waited until Natasha had grown old enough to take care of herself. He was sure she was OK. After all, Maishe joked with himself, what harm could a nineteen or twenty-year-old woman get into?

He had a sudden impulse to call her, his daughter. In fact, he was filled with an overwhelming dread. Maybe something had happened to her. Here he was, looking after one girl while deserting his own daughter. What kind of a father was he, after all?

He left his coffee and paper and crossed to the wall phone across the room. On the wall next to the phone, a bulletin board had clipped, stapled, tacked to it hundreds of business cards from previous visitors—most overlapped with care and precision, like the overlapping shingles of a roof. A few had phone numbers scribbled on their white and green and yellow and blue empty-spaces, clearly from callers jotting down needed numbers.

"Hello."

"Natal, Natasha."

"Dad? Dad, where are you? We've been worried sick. What—Where—How, Why—?"

"I'm all right, Natalie. I'm fine. I just—I need to get away for a while. The only problem is I miss you terribly."

"Daddy, I miss you. When are you coming back?"

"I don't know. I, whenever I, I don't know. I'll keep in touch, though. Maybe wherever I wind up, you can come to see me."

"Yea. Maybe."

He could hear in her voice she was crying. Maishe knew he would start crying soon. It never took much. He cried at those sentimental television commercials, the ones where the soldier surprises his mother upon returning home, the friends call each other over the phone after so many years.

"So you moved back home, then? I thought you might."

"Yeah. I don't know for how long, though."

She was crying now.

"Dad. Mom, I mean, she's so angry."

"I know, Natalie. She's been very angry for a long time. But I had to leave. I couldn't listen, are you OK? Are you eating all right? Sleeping all right?"

"Yea, I'm fine. I haven't told Grandma yet."

"It's all right. I'll call her. You just be well, OK?"

"Take good care of yourself, Dad."

"So far so good sweetie."

"I love you."

"I love you, Natalie. More than anything. Hang in there. things will get better. As soon as I…things will get better."

"Bye."

"Bye-bye."

He stood by the phone, holding it, cradling it a while, as he held her when she was his baby, until he heard the shuffling behind him, and he realized a fat woman, with spittle gathered at the corners of her mouth, stood waiting for the phone. Probably she had overheard every word. Well, it didn't matter. Like the doctor at the end of Three Sisters said, "Nothing really matters."

Yet it did matter; certain things mattered. It was clear to him the way he loved two twenty-year-old women—each in their own way, one known to him since birth and before, one known to him only a few days that some things mattered.

Amazing, Maishe thought, *just how thinking of Krystal infused energy and life into his manhood.* It wasn't as strong as when he had been twenty-five and thirty, but it was definite and would allow him to respond, he knew.

The door by the phone next to the bulletin board with cards was the door that led outside. The fat woman whose spittle gathered at the corners of her mouth opened the door that led outside and screamed, screeched.

"Sarah Jane. Sarah Jane."

From a distance he heard a shrill, younger female voice screech out, half in impatience, half in relief.

"What?"

"I'm goin' t' call Michael now. I just got the phone."

"What?"

"I just got the phone. I'm callin' Michael now."

"Well, call him then, we got to go…"

"I'm calling now."

She closed the door, muttered under her breath, and dialed the number.

"You get through to your daughter, all right?"

Maishe looked at the woman calling. For a moment he thought she had asked the question. Then he looked about.

The waitress was on the other side of the room. She looked harried, tired, overwhelmed. She was attempting to take an order from a family with two young unruly children. The boy kept pulling his sister's hair; the girl screamed and told her parents who told the boy to stop it; then, the entire parade sequence began again.

"Who…?"

"Here. Down here. I can talk to you now I'm cold and you won't drink me."

The coffee, Maishe knew.

"So. Coffee can talk, just like tomatoes and radishes. Apparently, organic liquids can slosh conversation about with the same facility as solid plants and vegetables."

"Well, why not? In fact, coffee has even greater stories to tell. Ah me, yes, the stories we know. And to think, you see, we never die, we always return, after a while, in another cup. Coffee, after all, like any liquid, flows with its stories, runs through a river of consciousness, channels a stream of tales and gossip, truths and half-truths, honesty and lies."

"So. Can you tell me about my future?"

"No. Nothing. I know only of what you tell me, or what I overhear. I then spread the news to other coffees through the slimy slippery sluice of knowledge."

"Well, then, coffee, prepare thyself. I've got a humdinger for you. You see, what is truth and what is a lie? For example, we are held to the earth by gravity; but, if we stopped believing in the force of gravity, who can say that we would not float about, being contained only by the confines of our ceilings constructed by those of us who continued to believe in the gravitational field. Well, a few days ago, the truth, or the lie, believe what you will, is, that I got up and I realized I could no longer live the life I was living. Now I'll tell it to you in detail, as it has happened so far."

After a while, Maishe Rosstein completed his story, up to the time he sat down to finish his coffee and began telling the story. Maishe got up from the table. He walked to the cash register. He paid his bill. It dawned on him that he was missing Krystal. The fat woman was still on the phone, muttering something about an overheated engine. He wondered if the coffee would find her story as interesting as his. He quit the coffee shop.

******

She stood by the bed, dressed only in her panties when he walked in. He gasped at her disfigurement and her beauty, for they were the same. He loved the thin, weaving scar, that flowed like a rivulet from her armpit over her right breast, just missing her nipple to the arm side then down her abdomen to just above her clitoris. It was this flowing stream of hardened female flesh he found that when he caressed it right and kissed it right and with love, drove her to fits of ecstasy—and, he had discerned, she knew how to use it to help men, too. She was free of hair for an inch on either side of her woman's opening.

"Maishe. Where have you been? I was worried. I was really worried."

She ran to him and he held her and felt her shudder.

"It's OK. I got some coffee. I read the paper. I do that in the morning sometimes."

"I, I guess I'll just have to get used to it, your—the way you do things and all, I guess."

So it was said at last. They were a couple. They had to learn things about each other's habits. Maishe felt good.

He held her close. After a while, he gently pushed her away.

"Krystal."

"Yes, Maishe." She looked up at him, her eyes glistening, sparkling, trusting.

"You remember what you said yesterday, about my tying your hands and making you do things?"

She smiled a wicked-happy smile. "Yes, Maishe."

It was amazing. Like a thirty-year old. He felt full of love and lust.

"Turn around and put your hands behind your back. It's time for you to be punished." *And loved*, he thought.

"Yes, Maishe. Anything you say."

Obedient, dutiful, deserving she knew of what was coming, she turned from him, and crossed her hands behind her back; and her hands rested just above her buttocks where another small scar ran to the right quadrant of her back—but the rest was smooth and firm and soft, like it was supposed to be when it belonged to a beautiful woman.

******

Later that night, he took her to a restaurant in a motel across the interchange. It was, he figured, about the best one could find outside of a large city. Later, if she wanted to, he could drive her through the town. Perhaps they'd stop at the museum. They hadn't done that, yet, like he thought they might.

The land had changed. It was the west, already, the old west. They followed the first loop of the old Oregon Trail, the course of the Platte River, that strange meandering, moving placid lake that altered drainage and reopened lost channels, that served home to myriads of wildlife native, transitory, and migratory. It seemed odd that cities farther west and along the way wanted to damn it up, destroy species of fish and fowl.

Hopefully, the people working against it—Nebraskans mainly-would prevail. This quirky river that ran due east needed champions.

Like that ancient river in Jean Auel's *Earth's Children* series, it was a great mother to life and national identity, and it needed to survive far more than a few suburban lawns kept in the immaculate form needed to survive for the sake of some warped, excessive, ersatz middle-class status.

He was pleased to recognize some of the old anger welling within him. It meant he was alive. But he had discovered that truth through other feelings the past few days.

"Good job," the cup of decaffeinated coffee said. Maishe sometimes liked to have a cup of coffee after a restaurant meal.

Usually, he had only one cup, in the morning. But occasionally he liked a second cup for a day after an evening meal at a restaurant.

"'Thanks. It's OK," Maishe said.

"What," Krystal said.

"What, Krystal," Maishe said.

"I thought you said something."

"Oh, no, nothing," Maishe said. "How is your spaghetti?"

"Hmm, it is wonderful. Delicious. It's—I never dreamed I could—God, my life is so good since I met you. When I think of what jerks might have picked me up I get all weird scared inside, you know—I sweat and I have to run to the bathroom."

"Finish your meal. Eat it all up. You need strength."

"Yes, Maishe."

Clearly, the fire had not burned her inside. Everything in the guts and plumbing seemed to work at peak efficiency.

The food was OK, Maishe thought. Obviously, Krystal had never eaten spaghetti at Grisante's in Omaha, or at that Italian restaurant in the plaza in Kansas City. Maishe had gone to KC on a few occasions, usually with his wife. It was interesting that his wife's best friend had wound up living there, and, usually, when they went, they did something with Becky.

Maishe had fallen in love with Becky years ago, the first time he met her, on a large midwestern college campus when his wife was attending graduate school. Through the years, as they all changed, his crush on her had only grown. Sometimes he fantasized about meeting her in a hotel room between Omaha and Kansas City, in St. Joe or Rockport, maybe. But he had never done it. *He should have gone to KC,* Maishe thought. Maybe. Becky, even with her children and husband, would have run away with him. He had asked her half-jokingly for years and she had half-jokingly always said yes.

"What are you thinking about?"

"Why, you, Krystal. Who else?" Maishe said.

She was improving. Already, Maishe thought, *in just a few days.* She spoke better, clearer, appropriately. She was more observant. Again, for the hundredth time, when she smiled at him with those sparkling eyes, he had the impression she was without blemish. The waitress, the cashier as they went to check out, other patrons had all stared at her as he was sure he had stared at her at first, but now he saw only her beauty and knew now what a woman, what a decent person she was.

The people in front of them at the cashier's stand took their time. There was a dispute concerning the bill. Maishe sighed. He stomped his feet. He tapped the toes of his right foot, shifting his weight to his left. Krystal fidgeted, hopping from one foot to the other. The couple's little boy, four or five years old perhaps, had wandered off, while they concentrated on the disputed claim. The child approached a display case across the foyer. The case contained on its shelves gum, cigars, notions. The case was small and light and seemed a bit overloaded.

Maishe knew about display cases. When he was a teenager his parents had owned and operated a small dry goods store. There had been many display cases. One or two had been portable, to wheel out for a lure onto the sidewalk in front of the store. Like the failed dreams of the business itself, the mobile sidewalk case had stood a mockery to futility. This case seemed to be a mobile one that someone had decided to use on a permanent basis. The child, Maishe noticed, pushed the case. Did he see it start to tip? He glanced at the couple. They and the cashier were intent on arithmetic while their child pushed at the restaurant's display case.

He looked at Krystal. She looked at him. She smiled.

"It's taking a long time," Maishe said.

"I don't mind, long as I'm with you."

He smiled back. Something caught the corner of his eye.

The case tipped over. The child stood underneath. In an instant, Maishe darted to the baby, placed his hands beneath the tot's shoulders, yanked him free, and dashed out of harm's way. The case came crashing down, shattering glass everywhere.

Maishe heard women scream behind him, but didn't turn, shielding the boy and his own face from flying shards with his back. Finally, it was over. One small bit of glass tinkled for a few long seconds; then silence prevailed over what seemed a freeze-frame moment in reality. The child broke the tableaux. The boy started crying for his mother. Soon she had recovered and was there, grabbing the child from his arms.

"Thank you," she said. "Thank you." Then to the boy.

"Come on, Kevin. Are you all right? Oh, thank God. Just wait till I get you in that hotel room. Let me look at you. No, no cuts anywhere. If it hadn't been for this man, oh, thank goodness you were here, sir, just what is the matter with you?"

Finally, they were outside, in the cool night air, just the two of them. The manager had seen the whole thing from across the room. He had given them their meals on the house.

Everyone still looked at them with admiration as they left, and a few heads were seen talking, gossiping in wonder about this odd couple, no doubt. The night air felt cool, moist, refreshing.

"Maishe."

"Yes, Krystal."

"I don't want to go for a ride. Take me back to the room. You were so wonderful. I want to do something nice and wonderful and fine for you."

It was sometimes a good thing, Maishe thought, *to take off and head west, through hot days and cool, refreshing nights.*

4

Beets and Plums

Yes, the land had changed. The tree lines had been reduced to rows, following creek beds and the odd flow of the Platte. One peered out to the horizon and saw only prairie and plowed land. This was the land Red Cloud had won for his people, keeping at bay the white invasion for nearly twenty years, the only Indian chief and native army to be that successful. Soon the land would give way to the land of pioneers and writers, Laura Wilder and Willa Cather, a great, western, heaving prairie that would, in its turn, give way to farmers and, later, passing from sublime romance to mundane thrills, to football fans.

Red Cloud, General Crook, James Butler Hickok, the Earps, all had traversed this land on their journeys west and north to the mountains or the Dakotas or Arizona Territory. Now, Maishe observed, trucks hummed with whining tires bringing messages and goods on their various errands, rolling over concrete ribbon swaths through the wild prairie, tamed pastures, and domesticated farms.

Maishe could never understand why these trucks came up behind your rear bumper, almost as if to run over you. Usually, he ran the speed limit, maybe a mile or two over.

He looked down. Today his speedometer quivered between 85 and 90 and this land of mystery and awe was passing fast on either side of him, the hedgerows of forest, the prairie grasses, the towns a half-mile or so off the road, and the farms. They whizzed by in a blur. In the distance of his rearview mirror, far over a hill, then gone again, like a vision, he thought he caught a glimpse of a flashing blue light. Well, it was about time.

He looked over at the girl seated on the right side. Her face seemed to have that same expression, a countenance she had during sex, when all her blemishes and scars seemed to disappear and melt into the fullness of her nature-granted beauty. Her lips were slightly parted. She panted, breathless.

"Are you OK, Krystal?"

"Oh, God, yes," she said, in her sex-laden voice. "Amazing."

He was frightened. She found it thrilling, breathless. She was young. He entered the youth of old age. He suddenly knew he was, in fact, speeding toward old age. For a moment, he felt old. The car dragged his attention back. Speeding along one of the nation's major interstate highways, with his breathless best girl by his side, her hair flying from the hurricane gale force wind by the open window, he began to feel young again.

He did find interesting, however, how well the Vega handled the stress and strain. He had known the engine was good and could probably rev that high, but the body was holding up all right as well. Yes, there it was, the flash of blue glittering light. Sun glints danced off cars behind him and in front, but the blue flashing lamp of the law enforcement vehicle was finally clear in his vision then lost again. For a long time, it would be that way—dancing in and out of sight, like a fickle girl you brought to a crowded party.

Sometimes, he lost the car in front of him. He feared it exited the highway before he knew it. It occurred to him suddenly he was a 50-year-old man zooming 85 miles per hour west south of the Nebraska panhandle, with a 20-year-old damaged beauty by his side chasing some ill-conceived vision and half-imagined dream. It had started well enough, that morning they rose about ten. They decided that it was time to move on. Before they left, they took breakfast in the coffee shop. In the shop, an older couple was having trouble ordering. The waitress seemed impatient with the old ones. Maishe knew it was a busy morning in a busy place; still, it seemed the woman could take a little extra time. He started to rise, to go to the table. Krystal said, "No, Maishe. Let me. You've already done so much. Let me this time."

Maishe sat back to watch. He felt as proud as a father even more than he did as a lover, as the woman who should have been beautiful—so beautiful she struck him as quite pretty even through the disfigurements—arose, crossed, introduced herself, sat down, and assisted her elders with their ordering.

Occasionally, she reached over, pointed at an item on the menu, smiled, waited patiently, explained again, then looked up and spoke to the waitress, smiled at the old couple again, and nodded to the waitress when she asked a question.

Maishe noticed that the waitress was calmer, more courteous. *Krystal did have that effect on people*, Maishe thought. First, there was the shock about her malformed flesh, then the shock and realization that this should be a disfigured person, ugly, but her beauty still emerged, then this strange, unexplainable appeal she affected everyone with. The girl captivated everyone around her. At fifty years of age, Maishe knew he was besotted.

There was only one problem. At one point, the elderly woman took out a cigarette. She lit a lighter, Krystal jumped back, a look of horror in her eyes as she gazed at the flickering flame. She watched it as though time itself stopped for her until the cigarette was lit and the flame extinguished. She recovered her composure. She continued to assist the ordering. She shied away from the woman's hand which held the lit cigarette.

"She's doin' pretty good, ain't she?"

Maishe knew at once this was said by the coffee he was drinking.

"Doing. Well. Isn't. Yes, she is."

"She's a piece of work."

"More than that," Maishe said.

"Damaged goods, though," the coffee said.

"More than what, Maishe?" Krystal said.

As usual, he had not fully seen her return. She had a way of sneaking up on a person at times. Now she stood up, looking down at him over the back of her chair. He suddenly remembered her last night, sitting over him, her breasts, clean white, free of tanning like the skin above, undulating like soft golden globes, her tiny white hairs casting minute halo glows upon them against the dim light from the half-closed bathroom door, and the one scar traversing her body, caressing her nipple, stimulating her to exquisite pleasure when he gently traced its path, all the way down and then into her darkest secrets. She smiled. It was the first time he had seen her smile outside of the bedroom.

"More than long enough in this place, angel-eyes. It's time to move on."

They moved to the door, to the cashier. They paid their bill. This time it went smoothly. Maishe again noticed the business cards tacked up in order. A tilling-garden company, insurance salesmen and saleswomen, trucking and hauling firms, a resume typing service. Some cards had notes, telephone numbers. The payphone hung close. They left the shop. They walked to their car.

Maishe was suddenly struck with the beauty of this area.

He gazed the far distance, unto the horizon of the big sky.

For an instant, he had to catch his breath, for the deep rolling clouds looked for a moment like the tops of the mountains toward which they headed. It occurred to him they were too far away yet to see the snowcapped majesties. It was a mirage.

This was Cather's land. The grasses rolled away, yellow purple to the horizon, tinged with the deep brown of rich rural soil. They were in the west. The land and the sky and the waters teemed with a sparse character of life all their own.

A wind came up. It blew Krystal's hair back. A girl quit the restaurant. She passed by them. Maishe saw the whining, straining truck turning the curve of the access road, heading a little too fast into the drive of the restaurant. Suddenly he ran, sprinted across the six-inch parking barriers, and got to the girl.

"Look out," Maishe shouted. He grabbed the girl's shoulders. He held her back. The trucker had already hit his brakes but the vehicle would never have stopped in time. Maishe looked at the girl. He saw she was only fifteen or sixteen.

"I...I didn't see." She looked around. "I didn't see."

This last she said to Krystal, who had run up.

"Are you all right?" Krystal asked the girl.

"Yes, I, I think so. I—you saved my life."

"Thanks, mate." That was the truck driver; Maishe noticed he had an Australian accent.

"Yes, she's fine, we think," Maishe said.

"I was going to my car, I mean my girlfriend's car."

"I...mean—and—well, I didn't—I."

"You're OK now?" Krystal said.

"Yes, I think so. I, I've got to go to my girlfriend. We're going—I've got to go."

And she ran to a red 1987 Chevrolet Caprice and got in. the car pulled out fast, its rear tires spinning on the gravel of the lot. *Funny,* Maishe thought; *you don't see many rear-wheel-drive cars anymore. Cars are almost all front-wheel-drive now.*

The girl Maishe had rescued had long dark, brown hair, a full face, not with wrinkles but with folds under her eyes that came naturally and didn't detract from her being young.

A blonde head sat behind the wheel. That was the only glimpse Maishe had. There seemed to be a third girl in the back. Then the car was gone, down the drive, and out to the freeway exit.

"Good job, mate. She OK?"

This last was from the truck driver who was crossing into the coffee shop. The wind swirled up, a blast from the Rocky Mountains, unimpeded across the prairie. Dust, papers, gravel, hurled dancing dervishes about them. Their eyes stung from the fine particles of prairie topsoil, eroded and carried by the breezes blasting full bore. Beyond the waving grasses, clouds began to churn, at once turning a bit darker and casting ray-beams of decaying magenta light off the reflected eastern sun.

"Yes, she's fine," Krystal shouted. The truck driver waved. He gave a thumb's up signal. *At that distance he would see only Krystal's beauty,* Maishe thought.

The clouds still fomented a great rolling mass, like mountains in the distance over a yellow and purple prairie sea, broken up by the rich brown row-currents of agriculture land, the concrete ribbon cutting a swath through it all and the whine and strain of car and truck engines filtering the soil-laden, dusty gusts of wind.

"Maishe."

"Yes, Krystal."

"No one ever called me angel-eyes before."

******

They had traveled on, in the Vega, a lime-green dot along a concrete path torn through yellow and purple prairie and brown-sod farmland. The clouds bunched higher and deeper in the distance, and, for a moment, as if the clouds parted to allow the vision, Maishe felt he truly could see the mountains, those great, majestic guardians of nature along the spine—row of the western Americas. The rows of trees and the hedgerows along the tributaries of the Platte continued, deepened, mostly off to his left now, which he found strange since the odd river meandered to his right.

A hundred years ago, Maishe thought, *men and women traversed these lands on foot, on horse, or on flat board wooden-wheeled wagons.* They rode from Helena to Dodge, from Casper to Tucumcari, St. Joe to Tombstone, El Paso to Deadwood, Laredo to Coffeyville, Topeka to Tucson. Las Vegas was a small desert oasis north of the Colorado River and if cowpokes gambled their wages, their money was tossed about in the shadowy flashing firelight at night's camp, guarding the others' ethics with a long ride's companionship and the fleeting close comfort of a six-shot revolver.

They were single-action guns and single-action men in those days, heavy, effective irons on the hips and in the saddlebags of men who rode through Indian territory and outlaw land, men and women who rode hard and easy from sunup to sundown, chasing dreams that coalesced in the flames of the flickering campfires by nights too short, and congealed in the shimmering mirages of distance by days too long.

Now, trucks and their drivers sped on through these lands, chasing only unrealistic mileage and hour schedules, while others hungered and thirsted for their products at their destinations.

"You're very pensive," Krystal said.

"Pensive. A quality word, Krystal," Maishe said.

"I learned it from you Maishe," Krystal said. "I'm learning a lot of things."

He looked at her. Indeed, she was. He felt good about it.

"Yes, I know."

"Well?"

"Maybe I was thinking about you, your scarred, luscious body."

"Maybe. And maybe not."

It was the first time Maishe saw her coy. The land had changed. The sky had changed. The waters had changed. Krystal was changing. Perhaps she was gaining self-confidence. He thought of Natasha. They had occasionally liked to play chess. He was a terrible player and she not much better, but she was learning. *How was she faring,* he wondered. For the hundredth time, he chastised himself for being a terrible father.

Perhaps, he should turn back, after all. He hadn't gone so far that what was done couldn't be fixed, repaired, put back together.

"Maishe. What is it? What's wrong?"

"What? Oh. Oh, nothing. Just a little tightness, a little muscle tightness, that's all. Sometimes, I drink too much coffee or cola. That's why I try to get drinks with no caffeine all the time. It's nothing."

He hadn't realized he had his hand to his chest. It suddenly occurred to him that whenever he thought of Natalie he felt a slight pain in his heart. He'd be all right. His doctors told him he had a strong heart. And he never smoked or drank. He'd be all right.

"Are you sure? Do you want to?"

"I'm all right. I'm fine. Really. You'll see. Tonight, wherever we stop, I'm going to do something special for you."

She giggled. He had not heard her giggle before. Like everything else about her, it was captivating. She was a fetching girl and he felt light-headed in love, a feeling he had not known for years, perhaps decades. She moved close to him. Again he sensed the familiar combination of odors—the strong, healthy, young femaleness of her, with that slight hint of sallow, charred, melted flesh, an indefinable sickly-sweet mystery. Oddly, he thought of the holy souls heading heavenward in smoke, out of Auschwitz and Bergen-Belsen. But at Sobibor the inmates had revolted, killed their tormentors, and set ablaze the entire camp, burning it to the ground. And Moses himself, in the passage, "Korah," found in Numbers, did he not use fire and earthquake to rid the people of the rebellious law-breakers?

But what law had the holy communities broken?

"Oh, Maishe," the girl sighed, dropping her head on his shoulder. He realized his hand was playing lightly with her pants, on the edge within the seam that flowed over the sweetness of her womanhood. He was astonished to realize he was swelling with anticipation of her. The clouds continued to gather into mountain heads.

******

He pulled off at the Kearney exit. He was half-way interested in seeing the campus, especially now since it was expanding to become a university. He thought perhaps Krystal too might be interested in seeing a college campus.

After all, she was the right age. She might want to attend an institution of higher learning someday.

It was not long, however, before he realized he had made the turn into the town itself and found himself on its main street. He was astonished, taken aback. To Maishe Rosstein, it was like a picture cut from the 1950s; here, in Kearney, Nebraska, life went on as it had throughout all of America for decades. There were small, friendly shops, with customers, passers-by, and shopkeepers knowing one another, an air of friendliness capturing each one: A small bank, specialty shops, a small JC Penney's, a shoe store, a dress shop, all facing the street, the old-fashioned look complimented by diagonal parking. Maishe suddenly realized that all through rural America, there were still vibrant towns like these, the same and yet with their own identities indelibly stamped on each main street.

He was somewhat surprised that so few students walked the town, browsing, shopping. It was early in the day, of course. Then Maishe knew the frightening truth. The clouds represented a gathering storm. They hurled and churned in a distance, a great mass of gray and silver, their peaks reflecting a sun moving graciously west, a little past overhead now, but it was all a forecast of the end. In time, even this remnant of simple times gone by would erode; a Walmart or a mall would open out, away from this town's center of commerce, and most of the merchants would fall into denial, a doomed stance, and the street, although it would never fully disappear, would erode.

It was the colors that struck Maishe. The dresses that hung in the windows on half-formed mannequins seemed to mimic the yellows and purples of prairie wildflowers. In fact, most of the patterns were floral prints. There were reds and greens, blues, and even an off-orange—burnt-orange, he believed they called it. The bricks of the street and buildings were dull, brown, and rust-colored; it seemed as if the colors of the clothes on display bloomed forth blossoms of flower-color toward the brick and macadam bouquet. But it was the shoe-store that snagged the girl-woman.

There were beige pumps on a glass-platform display in the window, the backs of the shoes, right where the woman's heels would fit, covered in a blue-red diamond pattern. There was a little silver line around the back of the heel itself. Maishe hadn't seen the little silver line around the back until the clerk brought the shoes out for her to try on. He was surprised he had been able to observe clearly the beige shoes themselves and their blue and red diamonds on the back of the heel, but the store was close to the street and the reflection from the sun off the clouds to the west had hit them right when they passed. The heels were about a half-inch or so. Pumps, he seemed to recall they were called.

He heard her breath draw in. He knew in advance what she was about to say. Again, glancing over at her, he realized that, when excited or interested, her malformed patch-work flesh on her face seemed to subside and present only the beauty originally designated for her. It was the eyes, he had no doubt.

Deep-set within the mask, when they began to sparkle, dance, gleam, and glitter, for him it was all over.

"Oh, Maishe. Did you see that? Did you see those shoes?"

"Yes, Krystal."

"Weren't they gorgeous? I wish I could—no, it would be too much to ask, wouldn't it?"

"It's all right, Krystal. We'll get them for you. Or something similar. It all depends if they have your size."

"Oh, I know they will. They must. They just must, that's all. I never had shoes like that. What are they?"

"Pumps, I believe they're called."

"Pumps, yea. I mean, yes."

"There's a dress shop two doors down. I'll buy you a nice dress to match, too."

"A new dress, too? Oh, my, I never had a store-bought dress before. A store-bought dress, and a new pair of shoes. Maishe, I think I like Kearney."

"First we check out the coffee shop. It's starting to get a little past lunchtime."

"Yes, I am hungry. But couldn't we first…"

"No. Lunch first, then shop. You'll appreciate it more."

"OK, Maishe," Krystal said. She had agreed, but he noted that she pouted a bit, her lower lip stabbing out, and with that, the pattern of her tragedy had returned.

It occurred to him once more he was acting more like her father than her lover. In some crazy way he could not fathom, a way that only the ancient Greeks might have understood, he knew he was both.

He pulled in at the diagonal parking spot. Along this side of the street, in front of this coffee shop and its neighbor stores, he noted that all the parking spaces were set at a diagonal, like you saw in those old newspaper photographs of the city market and downtown streets during the 1930s and 1940s.

He looked across the street. There was another cafe. On that side, the cars all parked in parallel spaces, like on most streets since the middle 1950s. He did a double-take, then saw he was right. The red Caprice pulled away from that shop's space. Through its rear window, he saw the blonde hair of the driver, the brown hair of the girl he had rescued in the passenger's side, and the third—was it blonde also, the head of the girl in the back seat? The Caprice headed out, back the way he had come.

After lunch, when they quit the restaurant, he saw a large Buick go past, down the street, inching very slowly. He could see it was the old couple, looking straight ahead, as if afraid to glance right or left, and the sun, with a ferocity he had not noticed from any other car, glinting off the border-chrome.

******

Out by Ogallala, they stopped for an afternoon break.

The clouds gathered no longer as mountains in the distance now, but formed a thick roof encasement, close. It seemed to Maishe like he and his girlfriend could reach up and touch the white, gray-streaked billowing ceiling.

"Lord A'mighty, Maishe, look at that," Krystal said,

She gazed out the window as they drove. "Lord A'mighty. The clouds look'n like you could just plain reach out and touch 'em. I never saw any clouds like unto those before."

Maishe realized at once the girl had suddenly become so awestruck of the majesty and glory of new-found nature, she had reverted to some of her old speech patterns without realizing it. He didn't feel like correcting her, however, so full of natural poetry had her speech been that no standard grammatical expression could serve so well the grayish, white-laden, black-enmeshed, silver-encrusted, golden streaks of the cloud breaks.

Suddenly, a wild western wind disrupted the calm ceiling-roof quality. The clouds swirled. The clouds clumped. The clouds jarred each other. Occasionally the clouds sat still, like polite crowded folks standing on queue for an important event.

Lord a'mighty, thought Maishe. *They are something. They do seem close.*

"A western sky, Krystal. Big sky country, as they say."

"Yea. A western sky. A western sky covered in a canopy of gray-streaked cloud; no, not covered; filled over—a western sky filled over with a canopy of gray-streaked, of silver, of a silver-streaked cloud."

And she repeated her full edited version, parsed to perfection. Maishe smiled. There was more to Krystal than the mystery of her mask could ever reveal. They turned in at Ogallala for a coke break. Maishe was sitting in the window of the small coffee shop when he saw the red Caprice pull in for gasoline. The girls must have stopped somewhere in town and were now returning to the highway. He watched the girls get out, the girl on the passenger side, then the one from the back. Yes, she was blonde, and even a little younger than the girl he had rescued. They pumped the gas.

It occurred to him that the driver had not turned off the engine. The girls looked around, first one way, then another. In the background, dishes and plates clattered, the usual restaurant syncopation. Waylon Jennings or Kenny Rodgers sang a mournful tune over the juke-box. Except for show tunes, Maishe didn't know, and, he felt, didn't really care to appreciate music and songs very much, the way most people did.

"Hmm, this Coke is just what I needed. Maishe, will we?"

"Krystal."

"What. What is it?"

"I don't know. Something's wrong. Something's going down. Get ready to…"

Maishe wasn't worried about the check. He had already put more than enough on the table. In an instant, he was up, dragging her.

"Come on. They've pulled away without paying for the gas. We've got to stop them. They're going to speed and get killed."

He stopped long enough at the cashier to tell her to call the highway patrol, that a red Caprice had just lifted some gallons of gasoline and that a green Vega was going to try to stop them. Krystal balked a bit, for the cashier lit a cigarette directly in front of her eyes. Maishe saw the look of terror in the girl's glistening clear blue eyes whenever flame reflected within them. She recovered as he yanked her outside.

Now, as dusk approached, here he was, fifty years old, hurtling down the highway like a bullet, 80, 90 miles per hour. They had turned off to the left onto 74, the expressway leading to Colorado, and soon, at the speed they were driving, entered the state. *So, that's how I leave Nebraska for good,* Maishe thought, *not with a whimper nor with a bang, but with the engine exhaust bellowing.*

Maishe was neither surprised nor concerned about the Vega's engine. It had always responded to the good care and service with which he had tended it. It was humming now, purring at 85 miles per hour. Mile by mile, though, as the markers and reflector poles whizzed by, Maishe detected a vibration in the body. He was certain the Vega was falling apart, disintegrating, the metal disassociating itself from its frame. In horror, he realized why he had detected no rust on the body all those years. The corrosion was all underneath. Like a bizarre horrible insect, the thing had eaten itself out from within.

In an instant, he knew, the entire affair would demolish, explode all over the highway and he and Krystal in it. That was when the saw the flashing blue light—wait—now there two of th—no, three, three patrol cars, and one of them as if from nowhere, directly behind him, filing the mirror, like a sudden close-up in a film, like a sudden dream vision.

Maishe breathed a sigh of relief. He could slow down, pull over. They could give the Vega a rest. He pulled over. Like a close witness on a race track, Maishe heard and felt the patrol cars whoosh by. They had their lights on but not their sirens. Almost from the instant they entered Colorado, Maishe observed that the land changed again.

The Platte had marched away to his north and the hedgerows and trees gave way to a gently rolling plain. Patches of green scrub grass formed a cross-patch pattern with the soil, brown here, not as dark toward black as in Nebraska. The quilt-patch form of the land reminded

Maishe of Krystal's face, only no eyes sparkled beneath the veneer of the rolling green, gold, and brown hills.

"Come on, Maishe. Let's go on," Krystal said. "Maybe we can see where they stopped them. The car's all right, isn't it?"

"The engine's all right. I don't know how much longer it will hold its body together."

He pulled out, on the slow lane of the interstate. There wasn't much traffic. Since he had turned off 80, he noticed that traffic had declined. He was sure it would pick up as he approached Denver. He didn't need to drive far. Driving only 50 now, and it seemed a crawl, he turned a curve, came over a hill, and saw them.

"It's a turn-off. They tried to turn off," Krystal said.

"They didn't get very far into it," Maishe said.

The Caprice had flown over a ditch. Maishe knew at once what had happened. The driver had turned off but had failed to slow on the access road. She had skidded, attempted to correct, and lost control. At 80 miles per hour, the Caprice had become airborne and cleared the roadside ditch. It had come to rest in a field. The three Nebraska Patrol cars were by the ditch, their blue lights flashing. Maishe saw two Colorado Patrol cars heading in their direction up the parking lane against the direction of the access road. Maishe stopped. The car screeched a bit.

The officers did not look up. They were intent upon their work.

"Oh, Maishe. I think those girls are trapped in their car. What…"

"Not all of them."

"What?"

"Krystal, what kind of field is that?"

"Beets, Maishe. Sugar beets."

"Beets. Sugar beets. Well, they just yielded a sweet crop."

Krystal didn't see the figure just outside the car, over her right shoulder. It was a girl with long brown hair, standing there, in shock clearly, a trickle of blood, deep-red like a beet running down the curl of her forehead.

Maishe thought of the ditty he had known and played as a child. It was his own record player. He loved to play the ditty over and over, with the sunlight settling in over the record player through a large picture window as he sat on a cross-patch tile floor. Krystal's face suddenly recalled the pattern of the tile floor.

'There was a little girl, who had a little curl, right in the middle of her forehead;
And when she was good,
She was very, very, good;
But when she was bad she was horrid.'

"Maishe, she's hurt."

"Well, let her in—help her in."

Krystal got out and helped the girl into the back seat.

The Vega's door was very large so it was not so difficult.

"I'll be mm—da—I—"

"Maishe, what is it?"

"Look, Krystal, up on that ridge. That lone tree. There's a little solitary plum tree against all this nothingness, a volunteer, small, ratty, but producing fruit."

"Maishe, it's raining."

And the storm had broken. Lightning crashed, yellow and white streaks above the flashing blue of the patrol cars. Maishe headed on into the town two miles down off the access road, past the scene of the crime, the officers still working over the car. Water poured over the Vega's windshield like a wash. Maishe realized he was keening softly.

"…who had a little curl…"

The girl in the back started to cry. Lightning bolts streaked and raced across the sky. Buckets poured upon them, a mighty deluge, forming great wall-sheets of hurtling water.

"Lord Almighty," Krystal said.

"Well, now you've got two of them," Maishe heard the plum tree snicker.

5

Honeysuckle

The car seemed to negotiate every obstacle. It plowed on, through rain, mud, snow, ice, highway chases at 90 miles per hour. The road, as far as he could make it out, had lost concrete or asphalt pavement and seemed graded with gravel.

It was difficult to tell where or what the road was, so intense the storm. All day it gathered; now, at night, it burst upon them with fury. Sheets of water washed across the windshield, giant drops pounded the long front fender of the lime-green Vega, then careened up above their view, to fall and split again.

Lightning so frequent and so intense as to confuse the passengers when dusk turned to day, then turned to night again, crackled and discharged golden slashes and amber creases across a darkly billowing canopy. The creases at times reminded Maishe of the long beautiful pattern the scars caressed across Krystal's body. For the hundredth time, he found himself wondering how beautiful she was, how astonishingly beautiful she might have been had the fire that must have been horrible not occurred.

"Lord A'mighty, look at that one," Krystal said. "Maishe, some of them seem directly in front of the car. I've never seen anything like it."

Maishe didn't answer. He was no longer sure if he was on the road or not. He tried to feel out the bevel in the grade, but the Vega began to fishtail—he was sure now it was rusting off its frame. He no longer knew how long the car would last.

Suddenly, two beamed lights appeared in the haze of rain and creeping darkness. The thing attached to the lights shoved past his side, missing him, he was sure, only by inches, splashing even more sheets of water over the side and front of the car. As it passed, he caught a glimpse of the bed of the truck. Maishe cursed the idiot driving the pick-up truck; Still, he was grateful to discover the Vega was indeed on the road into town. Although they were so far dry, Maishe had a sense they all felt wet, and, occasionally knew he felt small droplets of water.

"I never thought I'd be in an accident like that."

Krystal turned around. "Are you feeling a little better now, honey?"

Maishe jumped with a start. For an instant he had forgotten the girl in back. For the first time in a while, he chanced taking his eyes from the road to look in the mirror.

It fascinated him that Krystal, surely no more than three years the girl's senior, had, with the term, "honey," clearly assumed a parental tone and position. She would not soon allow her status in the car to be usurped.

The girl's face was not as long as he had first thought, a bit more to the round moon-shape some pretty girls have, although it might have been swollen a bit from the injury.

He had been right about the hair, though. It was brown and long and caressed the sides of her face. It was stringy now, wet from the storm, and it gave off that distinct order of wet healthy young female hair.

"What's your name?" Krystal asked the girl. She was turned around three-quarters, facing the girl over the seat. Maishe observed for the first time someone who did not reveal an initial shock at seeing Krystal close-up.

"Julia. I call myself Julia, like people to call me that. Perry called me Jenny. He hitched me up to a plow one time and made me plow two acres. It was hot and sweaty, my hair and back were perspirin'-wet, and my head and feet hurt. He said if I didn't do it he'd beat me again. He said I made a good jenny, and since I looked like a mule, anyway—well, when Sandra Sue said she was running away from home and would I want to go too, I come with her, me and Sandra Sue and Tammy Jo, We just took off. I hope they're all right. I never was in an accident like that. My brother, Junior got killed in one accident. State patrol officer said it's cause he wasn't wearin' no seat belt, but none of us never wore no seat belt, we thought they'd kill you and we didn't like the government telling us we had to. I think I might have lost a tooth."

"I think the town's just ahead," Maishe said. "I think I saw a light, a yellow light."

"How far did you come?" Krystal said.

"We left from t'other side of Council Bluffs. Sandra Sue stole her step-mom's Caprice and we took off. We was havin' a good time till we ran out of money when we was pumping that gas and took off, and you followin' us. We thought you was the cops."

"Yea, there it is, up ahead; a cafe, I think," Maishe said. "The town cafe. I think it's open."

"My given name's Jamie."

"That's pretty," Krystal said.

"I like Julia."

"We'll call you Julia, then."

"Has a ring to it. I ain't never gonna be called Jennie again. No sir. No, ma'am. No way."

"Here we are," Maishe said. "Honeysuckle Cafe. Guess the name of the town is Honeysuckle."

"A sweet scent," Krystal said.

"I think I chipped off a tooth," Julia said.

They entered the cafe, the middle-aged man and the two girls, the brown-stringy-wet haired one, and the ash-blonde one, holding a newspaper over her head so as not to get wet too much.

Maishe knew in advance what the cafe would look like: The long green-topped counter at their left side with about twelve red-vinyl topped stools, a few chipped and torn, revealing the stuffing of the stool; Along the right side stood some tables with red plastic tops and chrome liner all around (there was a subtle pattern in the table-top, and it was always difficult to determine its hue and value); A metal dispenser that allowed paper napkins folded in the center stood on the tabletops, pressed flush against the wall. Salt and paper shakers stood sentry on either side of the paper napkin dispensers, and, in front, like the honor guard leader of the platoon, an ersatz crystal vase that held a pink or blue paper flower. Providing a backdrop to the arrangement the menus nestled in a raised silver metal rack. The menus had little metal clips on the clear plastic book-form covers; Maishe knew that when he opened the menus he would see a typed list, somewhat difficult to read if he had by chance selected the eighth or ninth carbon copy, all reasonably priced specials, mostly meat entries.

The aroma of rich strong coffee and beef warmed up a half-day too long greeted them as they found their table, at the far back. A high wall rose across the divide of the restaurant, no doubt hiding the kitchen from the dining area, although the through-window from the waitress's counter to the kitchen was clearly visible. Metal coffee pots perked on a multi-coffee warmer. Maishe heard the faint sound of water running lightly but steadily.

The waitress, in a light green uniform—a little lighter than the Vega, Maishe thought—looked startled when they walked in. She had red hair, with an attempt made to set it in a perm, a bit of a short neck, to give her the appearance, when she gazed up, of having her head directly on her shoulders. She chewed gum, smacking and snapping it. Maishe saw that one of her front teeth was dark gray, almost black. She held her pad in her hand, but she didn't ask for their order. She wore a name tag that identified her as Carlene.

"I'm glad you all come in. I'm afr—goodness Lord, did you come in from the highway in this weather? No one's fixed that main road in so long."

"Tell me about it," Maishe said. "Some idiot in a pickup nearly washed me off into the gully."

"That'd be Junior."

"Junior," Julia said.

"Yeah, Junior," Carlene said.

"That was my brother's name. He was killed in a car wreck 'cause he wasn't wearing no seat belt, the state trooper told us," Julia said.

"The accident up on the highway? We heard—"

"No, it was another accident, some time ago."

"Well, I'm sorry about your brother, honey."

(It seemed suddenly to Maishe that every woman would take a parental tone with Julia), "But this Junior—well I wish he were dead, Lord forgive me," Carlene said.

"What's wrong with him?" Krystal said.

"He's the town bully, that's what is, ain't no man strong enough, guts enough, be a man enough to—they're all out— God, never mind, I said too much."

"No, go on," Maishe said. The smell of coffee and cooked beef and potatoes were making him hungry, but he wanted to hear the waitress's story, and he could see the girls were entranced too.

"He's my ex. At least, I want him to be. I told him to leave and leave me be, but he won't. I swear, if he comes back here—say, honey, you're hurt. You were in that accident, weren't you? Let me get a little Mercurochrome. I'll just be a minute. I'll get you some coffee too. I bet you can use some after being out in this here nastiness."

Carlene left to administer her duties as a nurse and waitress.

"I like her," Krystal said.

"I think I chipped a tooth," Julia said.

"Damn," Maishe said. He was glancing at the menu. "I haven't had a good roast beef and mashed potato supper in a long time."

Waylon Jennings crackled through the tinny jukebox.

Carlene returned and began applying Mercurochrome to Julia's forehead.

"Ouch," Julia said. She jerked her head away.

"Sorry, honey. I guess I got to hurt you to help you. I had a doctor tell me that once. 'Sorry, Miss Caruthers. I guess I got to hurt you to help you.' Hold still now. There."

"What was wrong with you?" Krystal said.

"Women troubles. He was all right. I got better after a while. How you feel, now, honey?"

"I don't know. I think I chipped a tooth."

"Well, there's no dentist in Honeysuckle. You'll have to go to Sterling. It's about 125 miles. Have to wait till morning, though. You won't be able to get back to the highway, now—oh, shit."

Maish heard the silence as Carlene stopped snapping her gum. Maishe saw Carlene's eyes widen, then narrow. He felt, as well as heard, the rain increase in volume. He knew before he turned three-quarter around in the booth, Junior had walked in with two or three of his cronies.

They wore red and blue ball caps, jeans stained in mud, torn, black boots, and big wide belts. *They seemed always to laugh when they talked, or maybe it was grunting,* Maishe thought.

Before he set out on his journey Maishe had taught English and speech at a small state college. There was a professor of history there whom he spoke with from time to time. The professor of history had an idea about language, linguistics, phonemic pronunciation, vocabulary, and class and positions in society. In a way, Professor Spence reminded Maishe of Henry Higgins, but Maishe's colleague, he knew, was going a bit further, for academe was, after all, different than anywhere else.

"It's these sounds, these reverberations that hail at us from the back of the room or across the way, or from the rear of the cafeteria. I say sounds, Maishe, for they're not words, grammar, syntax, parsed sentences, the stuff that separates us from the slime. They're often not even sounds, just grunts, heaves, chortles, perverse laughs. We hear them as 'Huh, heyah, ya'—I don't know, some semblance of identifiable phoneme I suppose, but loud, cacophonous, ear-splitting sometimes.

"I tell you, Maishe, we're losing our language. You're an English teacher or a speech teacher, more than anybody else you should understand that. Long ago I realized we had lost our sense of history; now I see the worst of it; we're losing our language. They're taking your language away from you Maishe, you mark my words. Tell me, is it getting easier or harder for you to publish your work these days? Harder, I'll bet. No one reads anymore. All we're left with are grunts, heaves, snorts, screams. Everyone in the world is grunting and screaming for attention and we do not know how to express ourselves. You mark my words."

"Belches, too, Frank."

"What?"

"Belches. For some reason, the grunters like to show how much and how deep they can belch."

"We're losing our language, Maishe. We'll never get our history back and now we're losing our language."

Now, Maishe realized, these were the very grunts, belches, snickers, and sneeze that emanated from this august group standing in the doorway of the Hyacinth Cafe, the grunter named Junior at their head. Then, with sudden speed, he could not have predicted Maishe saw her dash, Carlene, the waitress with the pretty long face, almost a horse-like face, but feminine-equine, sleek-beautiful and captivating, and with a little neck. She darted to her pantry behind the counter, reached down, and extracted the longest, widest butcher knife either he, Krystal (he later learned), and Julia (he later learned) had ever seen in their middle-aged and youthful lives. The dolt, named Junior, bumped his fellows, standing on either side of him, with his elbows. They emitted that certain series of snickers and guffaws that these men emitted that always reminded Maishe of locker rooms under decaying concrete and wood bench stadiums and the scent of stale, spilled cheap beer.

The waitress's bare bodkin glinted in the pale fluorescent-lit, charged atmosphere. Water drops dripped. Coffee pots perked. A refrigerator's compressor relay clicked; the motor hummed. One of the coke machine's faucets suddenly bubbled, then, just as suddenly, ceased. The compressor stopped, with an unnerving shudder. After a moment, a dish slipped in the wash sink singing a slight wet slithering clatter. Maishe heard Krystal's whisper break the ensuing silence.

"Maishe, there's going to be trouble. I know when trouble's coming. There's going to be trouble. Maishe, lover, we are in a jam. We are in a pickle. We are in a stew. We are in a, a—"

"—a tsimmis."

"What?"

"A pot of boiling carrots."

"Lover, whatever the vegetable, it ain'—it isn't looking too cool."

"My tooth hurts," Julia whispered.

"Quiet, angels. Nothing bad's going to happen here."

That was a line from The Maltese Falcon, *or similar to it. Close enough,* Maishe thought.

Maishe was regarded as a bit more than a mere film buff.

One of the courses he taught at the small southeast Nebraska College was media communications. He knew film noir well.

He had seen all the Humphrey Bogart movies, several more than once. *The Maltese Falcon* remained one of his favorites. Maishe never failed to be astonished at Bogart's delivery. That was the actor's strength, his power, the thing that set him apart from other actors, lesser actors, of his, of former, and of latter generations—that awesome sense of delivery timing, using the full power of language, of phonetic punch, of syntax prosody, of language as diction, character, thought, and plot. There was a certain lyricism to it, as if the actor had found the music subtext to the writer's scriptural notations and transpositions.

Maishe had made many blunders in his life; his largest was perhaps that he failed to pursue risk. Once, years ago, he had wanted to be a film producer and director, He had even had his application accepted to a prestigious southern California University film school. Somehow, he had not mustered the gumption to get up from his situation to go, and the thing had dissipated, like torn pieces of paper lost outside, blowing by in breezes and zephyrs, always just out of his reach, lost and withering with the wind. Now, here he was, fifty years old, trying to recapture lost youth and lost dreams. Really, it was absurd. He had a family, a daughter. He should turn back, go home, face it through, and live it out to the end.

For now, though, there was a more immediate and pressing jeopardy. Three dangerous men stood to his left as he faced the cafe counter, a half-crazed woman stood behind the counter with a quartering-knife, and he was responsible for the safety of two young women seated in his booth, the one, with a patch-crazy-quilt face from some earlier terrible trauma-immolation, pressing her fingers into his back.

Maishe was not entirely defenseless, or, at least, not entirely in ignorance as to what to do. Years before, just out of college, he had received a commission in the air force.

He had top-secret work. He had been in charge of the nation's highest controlled documents, the nuclear launch codes. He had received firearms training and self-defense training.

Already, even after all these years, Maishe realized he was scanning the area, making a preliminary mental image of how the thing would occur, grabbing in his mind things that could be transmuted into weapons.

He was astonished to discover he heard Sergeant Malfoni's gruff voice as if it were yesterday. "Remember, gentlemen—anything can be made into an effective weapon, a rolled-up newspaper, a shoe, eyeglasses, a belt, a cloth napkin—practically any object—just think of it and it will be seen, it will be done."

It was, Maishe now knew, the best time of his life. He was young. He was young and life still stretched in unending days and chances before him.

Now he was in the youth of old age, the old age of youth, and he had three strong young men to contend with and he didn't know if he was up to it. He determined that he would try.

"Girls," Maishe whispered, "Here's what I want you to do."

"Get out of here, Junior Mayville. I'm calling the— Chief Hays."

"No need, Carlene, darling.' I already tellin' Mack how it stands. The last thing he said on his way out of town was, 'Well, Junior Hampton Mayville, I reckon you can be Chief, then.' See? He give me his badge and all."

And he held something palm-size and shiny in his hand.

Maishe saw the despair and fear in Carlene's eyes.

"Now, darlin', give me the knife." And the lout started lumbering toward the waitress.

"Now, team," Maishe said, a touch of quiver in his voice.

It had been a long time since Maishe Rosstein was in a fight, and he was surprised at how fast he moved.

With his fork, he dashed across to the middle of the room and jabbed the one, named Junior in the back of the neck. The girls, as directed, dashed around to the server's station.

They picked up the coffee pots. They opened the lids. Quickly they climbed up onto the counter. As the other two approached, they hurled hot coffee, the brew splashing over the heads of the women's would-be attackers. All three galoots yelped.

They cried out. Maishe came around. He grabbed the machete from Carlene's outstretched hand. He turned. He stabbed the first one, then the other accomplice in the abdomen, just below the sternum. He had trouble pulling the immense blade out of the second one's intestines. It was a big man, and the man grabbed the shaft of the blade with ham-hock size hands and fell forward.

With dispatch, Maishe had to release his hand from the blade.

He had in mind to have it when he faced Junior. Now the villain lunged toward him and he had no weapon.

The lout's hand caught the top of his head and sent him reeling against the front door. He lay there, propped up as he fell, dazed. He thought it was all over. But the brute slipped in the rapidly forming pool of blood spurting from the stomachs of the other two, and he too lay there for a moment, stunned, as he peered into the eyes of his dying comrades.

Suddenly, Maishe saw the three women standing over the brute, striking, pounding, smashing, raining blow upon blow upon him with pots, skillets, knives, pans, mixers, forks.

The beast screamed an animal scream and lashed out at them, hitting Carlene and Julia. Krystal backed away. But it had given Maishe enough time. He lifted himself up. He picked up a chair, discovering more strength deep within him than he thought he had. He approached the man from behind as the lout stalked the girl. In an instant, he brought the chair down, hard and full. Again, the brute fell, tried to rise, and Maishe smashed him again. This time he lay still.

Blood and guts oozed over the floor. The women cowered in different parts of the room. One of the stabbed men groaned, still alive. From behind the counter water dripped. Julia somehow found her way into Carlene's arms.

Maishe suddenly realized he shivered, shook, quivered, trembled.

"Maishe," Krystal said.

"I. I'm all right," Maishe said.

"God a'mighty. I thought we were the gonners sure. God a'mighty. Maishe."

"I'm all right, Krystal, really. I'm ju—I got—I've got the shakes is all. Bad. Got the shakes real bad. It's funny. I…I can't even stop my hands from shaking. Look at that. Shaking completely on their own. I can't st–but I'm all right. I'll be OK. Are you, Julia—?"

"We're OK. We're fine."

"I, it seemed to be going slow at the time, like a scene in slow motion in an old black and white movie. Film noir. Slow motion. But now it seems it all went fast. Real fast."

"God a' mighty, Maishe, you was—you were something." "So were you, Krystal. Both of y—all of you."

"Well, Maishe," Carlene said. "I reckon you can be taken on police chief now."

Maishe Rosstein reached down and picked up the badge, lying on the floor. He held it in his hand, like a long lost, then found, at last, treasure. He realized he wasn't trembling so bad.

"It's what I've always wanted to be," Maishe said.

"I've got to call the state patrol," Carlene said. She lifted herself up. She suddenly realized that in the excitement the hem of her skirt had ridden high. She smoothed it down in order to cover her legs, returning to modesty's sake now that things were beginning to return to normal.

"Maishe?" Krystal said. She looked at him. She walked over to him. She put her arms around him.

"It's what I've always wanted to be," Maishe said.

"I'll stay too," Krystal said.

"My tooth's starting to hurt again," Julia said.

"Listen, everyone," Maishe said. "I think the rain has finally stopped."

And all he heard then was the sound of water dripping from a leaky drainpipe outside, until he heard Carlene's voice filtering in from somewhere deep in the back kitchen reporting the incident to the state patrol.

6

Plum

He held the rifle in his hands as he trained at the academy. It was an M-16. He knew he couldn't miss with it. Even at fifty-three now, his superior eye-hand coordination had remained with him. It had remained with him all these years.

His hair had washed away with time. His once muscular body had gravitated to paunch. Occasionally his hip went out on him.

Though he had hadn't had it checked, at least not recently, he knew he had suffered a slight hearing loss (after all, he had suffered Meniere's Condition for a long time). The Meniere's occasionally brought him up somewhat dizzy. He had grown long in the tooth (although the dentist in Denver he, Krystal, and Julia had gone to told him as long as he brushed and flossed he should be OK), His sexual prowess sometimes astonished him, and sometimes, it deserted him into a frustrating flaccidity.

There was an assortment, a litany of aches and pains that sometimes he could enumerate and sometimes he couldn't. But his eye had remained clear, at least for things distant, and his hand firm and steady, at least during the business ends of crises.

He had worked hard at the law enforcement academy in Grand Island. He hadn't been able to keep up with the physical training along with the twenty-year-olds and thirty-year-olds.

But he already had his appointment as town constable (everyone in the town and its environs called him "Chief"), and his instructors treated him with respect on the calisthenics field.

He had excelled in his academic courses, as he knew he would, both in legal theory and in procedures, in training. His classmates, all younger men first skeptical, then stunned, later proud he moved into fourth, then second place.

Now, he knew firearms and weapons; men and women he trained with developed a camaraderie. At last, he would need all his training, all the skill he could muster, all the judgment his years could bestow. He needed them all, and some reserve strength that he could only hope and pray would surface when he called upon it.

The day had started well enough, but he knew there had been something wrong for a long time. He had slowly been building an investigation. He had heard the girls' screams over the radio. "Maishe. Maishe, they're here. It's them. Ohh…"

Then, fainter, as if at a distance. "I do love you and Krystal so—no, ah—."

The sound of her voice still rang in his ears. He had experienced a funny thought. At least, she was able to scream through well set and repaired teeth. Maishe had spent a significant amount of money on Julia's teeth. He had to find her. He was responsible for her. He was responsible for them all. He looked up. He saw the plum tree, silhouetted against the darkening sky, alone, aloof, a sentinel over the prairie, a guardian over the interstate highway that shunted countless drivers on their journeys east and west.

"Well, Maishe," the tree said.

"She's just over the ridge you're on. Better find some cover though. They'll see you sure enough," the plum tree said.

Maishe knew where it was and what to do. Only last week he had found the stone bench in the small clearing down by the wood line on the brook that seemed to come from nowhere. He began writing his report.

Then, today, his world he had built over the last year came crashing on him.

"Watch it, Maishe. Careful," the plum tree said.

******

Even the first night on the job, he knew now, he had undertaken his investigation.

Maishe often woke at three or four in the morning, alert. Usually, he was unable to return to sleep till five or six One such night he left Krystal and Julia sleeping soundly. He could hear them breathing, slow, rhythmical. Julia had a deviated septum and, by this late-early hour in her night's slumber, had begun to snore.

Sometimes at these moments, Maishe walked about the small apartment attached to the station, with its two lockup cells in back. *It strangely reminded him of James Arness's (that is, Matt Dillon's) hoosegow in* Gunsmoke, *although it was more modern, albeit,* Maishe thought, *not contemporary.* It looked like it had been built in the '40s or '50s. The wallpaper, a blue rose pattern, cracked and peeled. Large blue roses blossomed throughout the paper. Small blue roses blossomed throughout the paper. Sometimes the large blue roses peeled. Maishe suddenly recalled Laura's line from *The Glass Menagerie.* Laura recognized Jim, her one gentleman caller, from their high school days. She recalled his initial malapropism. He mistook her pronunciation of "pleurodesis." He thought she had contracted (and always called her) "Blue Roses." Actually, there was a double misuse by Williams, putting even Sheridan's Mrs. Malaprop to shame. Laura mispronounced her own disease from the beginning. She should have referred to it as, "Pleurisy."

The plumbing worked. The stove worked. The heating worked. They were Maishe's main concerns. He wished to ensure that the girls, his prisoners, and he would be serviced by proper sanitation. He wished to ensure that appropriate meals could be prepared and served. He wished to ensure that sufficient heat would well up in winter, for it sure got cold all right out here in the rolling hill land twixt the great mountains and the great prairie. It was an old hot water boiler, with dials and ambiance indicating a comforting heat so sufficient Maishe often had to turn the thermostat down.

Maishe liked the old *Gunsmoke* TV show. As the years went by it became clearer that it was consistently well written, the characters particularly well-conceived and developed. His only regret was that everyone seemed to show only the later episodes, the ones with Ken Curtis as Festus. They were excellent shows and Curtis had demonstrated his ability as a fine actor by creating one of the western drama's most enduring characters; but Maishe wanted to see the truly great episodes, the early ones, the opening episodes, with Dennis Weaver as Chester and Amanda Blake when she was young and drop-dead gorgeous. It always struck Maishe a great irony, one of the most stunning tragedies the story of Amanda Blake's death.

Gunslingers, drunken cowhands, ne'er-do-wells, gross outlaws and kidnapers, Miss Kitty had survived them all, outwitted, circumvented, or been rescued by her hero from them all, but she couldn't defeat the microscopic enemy that doomed all in the path of those who were careless or unwitting, a great plague of our century.

Maishe often wandered about the rooms, listening to the silence, or, if a prisoner was paying his rent, to the deep disjointed breathing of a troubled man (on rare occasions, a woman) snoring. Occasionally, a car rumbled through town, having taken a wrong turn off the exit ramp, or heading through to join the country road at the other end for a supposed short cut to somewhere. About two and a half years ago, just a week or two after he had begun to discharge the duties of his office, Maishe Rosstein, without realizing it at first, had begun his investigation of the terror of Hyacinth.

******

It was about 4:00, that strange hour of the morning when even the worst insomniac begins to feel blessed drowsiness descend upon him or upon her, an hour when at last the hemisphere of the planet is quiet, still, peaceful, serene, and, for a brief time, the world seems natural, pristine, clean, like it was meant to be.

In this quiet corner of time, Maishe Rosstein felt happy.

He felt himself. He was a sheriff. He was a chief. He was a certified law enforcement officer. He had been voted in by the town by a margin of 417 to 63. He had passed his certification at the academy. His daughter had come to be reunited with him for his graduation day. It was a bit strange, of course, the three young women sitting in a row at the ceremony. As soon as word got out that two of them were not the old man's daughters, the other cops wouldn't let him hear the end of it. Even today, two and a half years later, if Maishe had a case that involved a fellow of his graduating class, he knew he was in for a ribbing. Tom Andrews of the Grand Island Police Department was the worst. Maishe could always count on Tom asking something to the effect of, "Hey, old man—keeping your girls busy these days?"

Maishe knew, however, that he could count on Tom and Sandra, his other classmate who stayed in the area, to crash through a door, to chase down a dangerous felon right with him.

He had settled into the job as he knew he would, and it fit him comfortable, like an old chair, an old suit, or an old couch.

From time to time his daughter visited him. Then there were three young women staying in the apartment attached to the jail. The strange thing was how well the three girls got on. One time, they went to Denver for a shopping trip together.

Maishe didn't ask Natalie about her mother.

One of the few things Maishe found he missed was the extra-long couch he had in the family room at his house in Omaha.

It was a magic couch, instantly transporting any early morning insomniac into slumberland.

Still, when the deal was struck, it was an all right deal.

Maishe had the jailhouse, the apartment, all lights and heat, the two patrol cars, the little radio dispatch cubicle in a cubby of the office, where the girls took turns fielding calls.

He had a couch brought in from one of the nearby farm's auction sales. Already, two and a half weeks into the job, he was of a habit of stealing out of the apartment at three or four in the morning, walking about on foot patrol the three and a half blocks of the town, and returning to the new-found comfort of his couch in the office, falling off about 5:00 or 5:30. There Krystal or Julia would wake him with coffee about 9:00 and, by 10:00, he was on the job again. It wasn't the same as his old couch, but it served him well enough—that and the night air away out beyond even the dreams of city life.

Often, Maishe would stop in the center of the road and look about in the darkness, that deepest and coolest of darkness just before the glare and glory of first light. He doused his flashlight. He became enveloped by the majestic blackness of it all—broken only by the myriads of stars shining and twinkling messages of peace and hope, the only other light that of the jailhouse window, spilling into the street down the way.

Occasionally, he heard the rumble of a large truck out to the interstate. Mostly, it was quiet and peaceful and only a high-born owl's skree, announcing the bird's returning from a successful hunt broke the window-lit, star-lit silence.

Maishe returned to the office. He slept there on the couch, feeling a bit that that was what Marshall Dillon or Chester or Deputy Festus might have done, when they were on watch in Dodge.

******

It was such a cooling summer's night and crisp early morning that the incident had happened. He had just returned from his insomnious and solitary foot patrol. In fact, in later months, and, now, even two and a half years later, Maishe realized that had the affair occurred only a moment earlier, things might have been completely different. Of course, he also might not be here, stalking the bastards, hopefully, to catch them by surprise. He had been outnumbered that night too, and he would have been the one taken by surprise.

It was about 4:45. He had removed his clothes. He had turned out the lamp. He had crawled under the comforter he kept on the couch for this purpose. It was a warm night. Soon he removed most of the blanket to let his body cool. Behind the door of the room, leading to his two cells, he could discern the distant snoring of his one prisoner, a drunk driver, whom Maishe had pulled over on a chance patrol.

The guy was barreling down the entrance ramp of the interstate, heading the wrong way into the town. God only knows how he had made it on the highway. The records out of central had indicated a fifth offense, and the guy had no license.

Now he was sleeping off his dissolutions and his sins, but, in a few days, he would have to meet his consequences.

Maishe sighed, frustrated by the redundancy of capturing repeat offenders, ready to feel captured by the magic of the new couch and the tranquility of the hour. He felt good thinking perhaps he had saved some unwitting person's life.

He felt he was just drifting off.

Somewhere, in a nebulous world between wakefulness and slumber, he heard the car.

It didn't screech to a halt but there was something about the way it stopped and the opening of its doors that snapped him back awake. He padded over and looked out the window.

A girl, no more than ten or eleven, was running toward him. A man and a woman chased her. About halfway they caught her. She screamed. Maishe leaped back. He had never heard such a scream.

He returned to the window. He looked out again. Struggling, they returned to the car. Maishe's tired eyes recognized an old 70's black Cadillac. Quickly he returned to get his clothes on as fast as he could. The hint of drowsiness wouldn't fully dissipate. It hindered him from moving as fast or as true as ordinarily, he would. He realized suddenly, like a dam had broken, he needed to urinate and wouldn't be able to take the time.

Finally, he was ready.

Too late, Maishe thought. *Too late and it's worse than never.* Still, he thought it worth the effort. Sometimes, once in a while, he had been taught at the academy, cops got lucky.

The door to the apartment opened. He knew it would be Krystal. Julia could sleep when a freight train thundered past her bed.

"Maishe, what is it? I thought I heard something, but I couldn't tell if I was dreaming."

"Stay here. I've got to check on something. I'll call in on the radio if I need help."

Finally, he was out the door, shaking away the last dregs of near—sleep. As an afterthought, he dashed back in and grabbed the rifle, the very one he carried now two and a half years later, and which he always kept loaded. It was this afterthought which he later regarded as a great irony. It might have saved his life if it had come down to it, but that extra few seconds might have allowed his prey to escape.

The Plymouth Acclaim roared to life (it always started right away in the warm temperatures) and he was off. It was no use.

He covered the country roads for an hour, but there was no sign of the black Cadillac. Perhaps it had backtracked on him and escaped out onto the interstate.

It was pitch black except for the stars, the headlamps of the car, and the occasional farmyard lights, sprinkled about the land and rolling hills like a sparse expanse of fairy glitter. By the time he gave up and returned yellow washes of light whispered through curtains in the bedrooms, kitchens, and bathrooms of the old farmhouses, and

Homer's rosy-fingered dawn poked its fingernails above a broken horizon. The first hints of an aqua-pale blue sky rose above the pink line as Maishe headed back to town.

About a half mile before he entered the three and a half block village, his headlamps played a glare in the road. Maishe stopped the car, He got out. He bent down. He picked up the object. He held it in his hand. It was a metal dye, cut in a circle with zodiac symbols all about it. In the center was an askew five-pointed star with more symbols on it, Egyptian it seemed to him.

Maishe Rosstein looked at the pentagram for a long time and played over it in his hand. By the time he returned to the car, he could turn off the headlamps. It was clear day yet Maishe felt a chill he had not felt in the cool morning of the late night. He felt something else too, a vague uneasiness that he had stumbled on something important and that something was rotten in the city of Hyacinth.

He found Krystal half-asleep on the couch. She ran to him when she heard him come in. He didn't respond to her hugs or her plaint. She backed away. She had never seen him like this.

"Maishe. What is it?"

There was a distant gaze in his eyes.

"Maishe, you're scaring me."

"Krystal, something's rotten in Hyacinth. I found this."

"A star?"

"Yes. It reminds me of something I saw once, but I can't remember where."

"Maishe? Maishe, do you feel all right?"

"What do you mean, Krystal?"

"You're shivering so."

And she reached out, and pulled his head to her bosom, the way countless women had done to give their men comfort throughout the millennia when the men had suddenly been reduced to scared, frightened children seeing monsters in their bed-chamber closets. For the first time since they had known each other, she felt the mother-parent and he the child. And they stayed like that, an icon, for a long time.

******

But for these moments, and soon enough, Maishe realized, for the most part, he enjoyed a sinecure. There were the drunks mostly, out of the tavern or down off the interstate.

Occasionally, there was a domestic problem. Once in a while, he had to run an emergency to the hospital in Grand Island.

Generally, though, Hyacinth remained one of those countless sleepy small towns that dotted the American rural landscape, a town with a vision once which had never been realized and somehow hung on, with few hopes and little dreams, a place where the unambitious could get through their years played out in blissful futility and anonymity.

Once in a while, there was a job with a felon sighted between Omaha or Lincoln and Denver, and he would be called to assist. He looked forward to those moments. Still, he relished the tediousness and boredom of a job where little policing was needed. Boredom was good; after all, it was a Chinese curse that said, "May you live an exciting life."

He was regarded well. He was considered the best police officer Hyacinth had ever had. By 1:00 or 2:00 he was done with his day patrol. He headed down the street, passing the feed store, Maguddly's E-Z Market with its gas pump, the Hyacinth Cafe where it had all started, Willy's Tavern and Wiley's Bar, across the street from one another, the small post office with Jane Makimes, a half-Santee as Postmaster (open 3 1/2 days a week), the local bank, a couple of buildings closed and boarded up, the offside street, which led to about 30 houses in a four-block area and, on beyond, a Methodist church, and a grain elevator by a railroad spur.

Town legend had it that if you continued on past this end of Trails End Road, and a person could find the right path, he or she might find the old Wellstein Silver Mine in the Rolling Hills. Kids sometimes tried it in the summer, but usually found Ol' Blue Hole first, a wash eddy off the creek that got about seven feet deep in early spring and served as a swimming area.

Maishe sometimes ventured out to Ol' Blue Hole. It became a ritual for him, and a rare fresh town story about the new constable, to admonish a boy or a girl not to jump off the embankment. So far he had been lucky; no child had drowned on his watch. Then he returned to the only real intersection in town, turning left, where the main street turned to gravel grade; he drove into the county and farm roads of the surrounding area. Occasionally, if no other vehicles were coming, he stopped where he had found the pentagram. He would exit his vehicle.

A row of hedges stood by the side of the road, like a troop at attention, saluting a passing inspecting general smartly. From time to time a flock of quail paraded through the row, the one behind following precisely in a zig-zag fashion where the one in front had ventured, an age-old imprinted survival line of follow-the-leader. Beyond the hedgerows, a tree line marched alongside the creek bed. Once in a while, on a dry summer's day, Maishe ventured into the tree line.

He wasn't sure what he was seeking but he knew he'd know it when he saw it. Once he found a torn blanket, ripped to shreds and a frayed rope from a branch in a tree. There was an old campfire area.

He stumbled across some empty tins, other waste, and trash—at one time a hobo camp no doubt, off of the grain train spur.

He noticed a path off the area, which he always meant to pursue some time; but he didn't want to venture that far from the car unattended. Later, the drowsiness of the day, the lassitude of the season, the dreariness of the town, made it seem like too ambitious a project. Hyacinth could do that to a man, or a woman.

By 1:00 or 2:00 he entered the cafe for lunch. Sometimes Krystal or Julia joined him, the other girl monitoring the state patrol dispatch. Carlene always served them. By 3:00 or 4:00 he was back in his apartment for a siesta till 5:00 or 6:00, while one of the girls watched the office and kept an eye on the town. After awakening, he took a ride on the interstate 15 miles up and back in either direction; about 8:00 they'd settle in for a supper and the evening.

The girls took turns cooking and monitoring the radio.

On Sunday Maishe fixed the meals. He developed two rules for supper—prisoners got served first, and little or no shop talk was allowed.

In this way, two and a half years passed. There was one thing he always did. He always kept an eye out for a late model black Cadillac.

******

It was full night now. The chill of the winter solstice darkness enveloped him. Occasionally, he hit a wayward branch or stone. Only rarely did he use his flashlight—if there was a deep shadow, or if he felt branches and sensed he had wandered too far off the path. It wasn't that there were many trees in these woods—there weren't—not like Kentucky, that was sure but he wanted to follow the tree line and not be seen.

The surprise was his best chance—who knew how long it would take Tom and Sandra to be contacted and to head out, how much longer it would take them to follow his directions.

On more than a mere hunch, he followed the path he had found over two years ago. When he discovered it wound out beyond the plum tree on the hill, he was not surprised. The interstate was much farther away out by this side of the hill. The path headed even deeper into the enduring internal and ancient eternal mystery of the small wood.

As he slipped and sledded increasingly, Maishe began to realize the path was an old dried tributary of the creek, damned out dry when the roads of the town were built perhaps, or the spring had played out, sapped dry from the pivot irrigation units relying on table and aquifer water all around the surrounding counties.

It didn't matter. He was also afraid he wouldn't be surprised at what he found at the path's end, deep in this tree line. He'd pretty well had it figured out, and was building his case. *Fool that he was,* Maishe thought, *not to consider the coming of the winter solstice, not to figure they would hit right at his heart.*

If anything happened to her, he knew he'd kill them all. All his training would be forgotten. All his ethics of legal justice would be tossed aside. Only righteous vengeance would prevail.

He'd kill them all. Like the people sent into the land by Moses, to eradicate the offenses that were stenches in the nostrils of the Lord, the offenses, the sins, the horrors of child sacrifice and temple prostitution, he, even he, Moishe *Pinchas ben reb Yitzhak haLevi*, and not an angel, he alone would track them down for the rest of his life; he would kill them, everyone, the stench-producing bitches and sons of bitches.

Slowly, painstakingly, he built his case. Once, off the abandoned campfire, in an oblique direction he had not gone before, he found a bone.

Eons ago, in the days before so-called civilization, bones of animals dotted all the lands of the earth. Mass heaps of them washed up into stacks and hillocks at elbows of creeks, rivers, eddies. People collected them. People used them for tools and to build structures. Somehow, animal bones weren't found so much, not for thousands of years, and Maishe shuddered when he found this small bone. He knew before he sent it to the lab it was human, and, judging from the size of it, very young. When he knelt down to pick it up, his fingers began to feel like they were on fire. They burned. He sprinted to the car. He retrieved his water bottle. He poured cool water over his burning fingers. In the trunk, he had a uniform crime lab box. There was a pair of tongs and a plastic evidence bottle. He took them back where he found the bone. Something bothered him. He thought he had heard something, a rustling in the bushes of the glen. He suddenly felt he was being watched.

His hand instinctively fell to the .357 magnum he wore on his hip. With his hand on his revolver, he spun around.

He peered carefully. As if by command some pheasant rose from a small gully at a distance, their wings beating the air. Maishe leaped up in place, nearly as high as they flew. He thought about investigating over by the gully; instead, he bent down to retrieve his evidence. But he took a while, for the whole time he kept his eye over by the gully the birds had suddenly quit. He backed away. As he had been taught, he circled about like a slow spinning dervish as he made his way to the car. Ten days later he received the report from the Denver lab. The bone was the rib of an infant, perhaps four to six months old. The tissue of the bone had been treated with a very caustic acid. While he read the report, Maishe rubbed his fingers. They had been sore for days. In fact, they peeled.

Occasionally, they still itched and tingled. As he read the report, the image of the girl running toward him from the black Cadillac, the man, and the woman catching her, sweeping her up, it all flashed before his eyes. Suddenly he knew where he had seen the image of the pentagram.

The very night he had entered the town, he had nearly been washed, swept off the road by the rusty-green pickup truck driven by Junior and his boys, the same oafs he had to accost at the cafe. He realized now, perhaps for the first time, that in a flash of lightning, their ghastly faces had been revealed to him, and on the side panel of the truck's door, there had been roughly drawn a circle with a pentagram inside it, slightly off-center.

The state police investigation crime lab unit descended on Hyacinth for a few days after the report from the lab came back. But Maishe began to concentrate on Junior and his friends.

At that time, in the early morning hours, he drove around in his patrol car, looking for any farmhouse where lights would still be on. He could never pin his suspicious hopes on any one place, illuminated or dark. Then, about six months ago, he got the lead he sought.

******

For some years, law enforcement officials in cities and counties across the country had been getting word and accounts of cattle and other animal mutilations, of missing children vanishing without a trace. Evil was afoot in the world and this time it seemed to wander and roam unchecked.

Maishe Rosstein knew now that he had known all along he would have to look the face of evil in its eye and spit there.

He had known it since the day he drove into Hyacinth on rain and wash-swept road, nearly runoff by a mean green pickup truck with a crude pentagram on the side.

"Cops get lucky sometimes and sometimes you play your hunches to make your luck," one of his instructors at the academy had said. Soon after he had found the bone, Maishe remembered another incident from long before he was a police officer.

Few of these groups had been caught. Occasionally, county sheriffs got lucky. The Nemaha County Sheriff got lucky and called the Nebraska State Patrol. Although they were too late to save a child and a young man from hideous torture-slayings, they had broken the group in Rulo.

On a hunch, on a long shot, Maishe had contacted some of his instructors in the state patrol. They had opened some of the Rulo records and sent him copies. Night after night, at three and four in the morning, he had poured over the court records, the indictments, the police reports. There was a telephone record with a Denver telephone number, the number had appeared twice on the record. Incredibly, Maishe realized, no one had tracked down the record. Or, maybe, they had thought nothing of it. It was, after all, just a bank. Perhaps the group or some party simply wanted to see about interest rates on the cache of money they were gathering. But Maishe went one step further. He traced through DMV the automobiles of all employees of the bank.

The Executive Vice-President for Investments owned a 1977 black Cadillac. It had taken two years but now it all came together. He had gotten word Junior had been paroled from prison, nine months ago. He had always wondered where these groups got their money. It was suspected and there was some evidence to indicate that there was a sort of national network. Michael Ryan of Rulo, his Junior of Hyacinth, T. Robert Sanderson of Fidelity Denver, the unknown woman—Maishe Rosstein now knew the faces of evil, and now that he knew and suspected they knew that he knew, he had waited for them to come for him.

They had tortured and destroyed 15 million in World War II, 20 million in Russia since 1917, countless hordes of corpses before and since, and, in this little corner of the world, he, one man, chased them, and he knew they were after him.

But, fool that he was, he had not considered they would take him this way, taking one close to him. He fingered his badge. *To hell with the law,* he thought. If he had half a chance, he'd riotously, in righteousness, full of vindictiveness, murder them all with malice aforethought.

There was one thing Maishe hoped he had on them, one thing he hoped they had neither suspected nor learned. He knew their pathways. For six months now, since he began putting the final pieces of the puzzle together, he had been traveling the back paths and trails off the gravel country roads. He had found the old deserted Crawford place. He was sure he had found it, the long-lost log and clapboard house of the first settlers in the region.

The legend was they had all been carried off by Indians and the house was out there somewhere. He had found it, what was left of it, that, and gruesome pieces of evidence around it. And he had set up a surprise.

******

Now, here he was, 52 years old. He should have stayed in Lousiville, joined the police force there when he was 28. He'd be retired now. He's been living with ease on a pension.

Instead, he was 52 years old, overweight with a heart arrhythmia, tripping and sliding through some night bush, about to engage in the fight of his life. He was scared but there was also a sense of anticipation, of longing, hunger, need, desire, lust. His senses were aroused. He felt near to death. He felt alive. He felt young.

He rounded the last bend in the overgrown trail. He slid out into a small clearing. He crouched behind the old decrepit lean-to barn. It seemed that from directly alongside his kneeling position a calm zephyr blew up, caressing his head and the back of his neck, gently flowing across the clearing.

He felt the coolness of it, knowing now he was a flesh-bag of sweat and not from the untoward heat of the warm winter's night. He closed his eyes. He took a slow deep breath. He peered around. They were there, around an altar, a large slab stone. He knew who lay upon it. Oddly, he thought of her teeth and all the dental work he had paid to have it done.

******

It was all wrong. His whole life seemed a jumble of poor judgments, the one leading, hurling at times, headlong into the other. Exercises in futility. One should always return to one's home town, build a life. All he had done was lose everything. Only five months earlier, he had lost his mother.

The house and all the possessions, all the memories, were dissolved now, lost forever, gone with the wind, as Ms. Mitchell so aptly entitled her brilliant opus. What was left? The money? It only made life tolerable.

It could not change the past. Perhaps, he should be the sacrifice tonight. Yes, that was it. He would rescue the girl, kill them all, and one of them, with a knife or a bullet, would get him. It would be better that way. In the world to come, he would look down on them in hell while he sat by the footstool of the throne next to his beloved mother, and his terrible aspect would chase them for eternity through all seven of Satan's lower levels. Eon by eon, he would rise to the crown. After seven times seven eras, four worlds blinding in light, and four worlds enshrouded in mystery upon mystery, like Moses, Caleb, Joshua, David, Daniel, Akiva, he might even be one of the few granted the grace to see God's holy ineffable glory. Fire blazed in his eyes. This fire sparkled. This fire crackled. The Welling up of the flames, their dancing, and prancing, their twirling and spinning of red and yellow tips played like facets of pure diamonds, rubies, opals, sapphires upon the dark-robed specters about the nude figure on the stone.

She was, of course, terrified. She tried to sit up. He saw a hint of something else as the light from the fire caught her eyes. There was an eerie confidence, as though she knew he was there, or would be coming. The scene had played in his mind a thousand times, like a movie where John or Clint had come in just in the nick of time to rescue the damsel. But this was no movie set and he was not now nor ever would be a Waynian or an Eastwoodian hero. There would be no yells of "cut" if it did not go well, no retakes, no breaks with fresh orange juice in Monument Valley while the director and crew prepared the set-up.

If you were killed, you were dead. No rhetoric could argue against that premise. There would be no miracle resurrections. It was time. That bastard Junior raised up the knife. They stood around her in a circle. They chanted the non-prayer trope of the black mass. Hooded or not, he knew who the monster was. He knew them all, with their cloaks on or off, these good people from Denver, Omaha, Lincoln, Kansas City, Phoenix—the banker, the obstetrician, the judge, male, female, he knew them all, so carefully had he followed his leads. Only one, the high priestess, standing next to the bastard. He couldn't ferret her out, and he couldn't see who she was now. Soon he would know the entire truth.

It was time. This was it. His palms moist, his chest aching from fear and quivering from a fifty-two-year-old irregular heartbeat, he pulled the M-16 up, adjusted the scope, and let go two rounds, just as he had been taught. The man fell away, the knife flying into the fire behind him. He knew he had only a few seconds. He had to drop as many as he could. They were 13, 12, 11, 10, 9. They were still eight to one, and he knew the fog of battle would soon take over to envelop him.

The flames took on a life of their own. He heard footsteps, screams, yells. He thought he saw hooded figures running into the woods, toward him and away from him. In and out of the light they swam, like a kaleidoscope of shadow-puppets undulating against a large screen. He thought of the old barker expression, *now you see it, now you don't. Don't bother me, kid, I've got a hot one. Now you see them, now you don't. We've got a real hot one here. Round and round she goes, where she stops nobody knows.*

Any minute one of their bullets would catch him. He could see the blaze from their muzzles. Occasionally, he could hear the whine of the bullets, missing him so far, missing him so near. How long could the misses last? Suddenly, two appeared in front of him firing madly. He reckoned it. He fell to a supine position. He waited for them. Seven, six. How many had run off? Only one gun fired in his direction now. Carefully he took aim at where he thought the last muzzle blaze, the last bullet had come. He squeezed the trigger. A figure, grotesque in a spastic outline, leaped against the flames, danced a terrible twisting agony in the air, defying gravity, looking strangely like a crucified ballerina. There was silence, except for the fire, weakening now, and the girl whimpering at times, attempting a hoarse whisper, "Maishe?"

He dared not answer. He waited. How long since the whole thing had started? It seemed an eternity. He chanced a glance at his watch. Only four minutes had passed. When he looked up, he knew she was behind him, rising out of the morass, a hooded specter, a cloaked harpy, an evil Valkyrie, like death always stood only a step away from each of us, peering over our shoulders, waiting for its appointment with eternal patience and vigilance. *Do I have an appointment in Hyacinth this night?* Maishe thought. And then, as though one of the flickering embers shot a lightning bolt across his brain, he knew at once who she was.

"Thomas will not be coming with the backup."

"NO."

"I thought you were my friends."

"Don't fault him. He's dead. I had no other way. He was a good cop. Well, I guess, we all were."

"That's why no one's ever got a lead. You were there to interrupt traffic. You picked up on everything. Sandra—you, a whole network of you…"

"Shut up, you fat old man. How they ever let you in the academy. Now, look what you've done. You ruined everything. I'm going to keep you alive long enough to rip both your hearts out and eat them in front of you while you still know what's going on."

"I'm old, Sandra. You just said so yourself. Mine won't taste very good, I'm afrai—"

"Shut up."

Countless times he had raised her voice on the radio. Countless times he had chased thieves and rapists with her by his side. One time, they had felt the fury and the fellowship of surviving a shoot-out together. One time, they had driven their cars in tandem in a chase across the Colorado-Nebraska plains. Now there was a different person in front of him. A twisted ogre towered over him, hideous instead of beautiful. Julia's cries echoed across the deserted clearing.

"Maishe, save yourself."

"Sandra, in about twenty seconds, this barn behind me is going to explode."

"Liar. Prepare thy end!"

She held the automatic pistol to his gut. In that instant, he knew it was all over. Then, in that same instant, her face transmuted again. At once the beautiful police officer, the partner he had known, the comrade for whom he had risked his life and she for his, she now stood above him, her arms outspread, as though floating on gossamer wings, like an angelic visitor cast out to earth's vale of tears, her countenance curious about her fall from grace.

"Maishe?" She cried out in wonder and gently floated to fall at his feet.

He heard her murmur, "I'm so cold." And he saw the light of the real truth. A knife up to its hilt rested in her back. A foot or two away a slight girl with a scarred face stood.

"I had the hardest time finding you, Maishe. I wasn't sure. All the time I wasn't sure. Then I saw the fire. I almost ran away. My God, the fire, Maishe. But I got here just as just as…"

"Maishe? Why, Where, Who—How—when—?" She was still alive.

"Sandra. Soon the barn will explode. I set it up days ago. It, it's all over for you, Sandra. You know it. We've seen it before. With your last breath, Sandra, look to the light. Look to the light, and you…you'll regain yourself. Krystal, we've got to get out of here."

"The light. Yes. Save yourselves. For me, it's over."

They ran. They sprinted. Suddenly, there roared behind them light and heat and flame. They lurched down on the ground. Missiles of fire spikes hurtled past them. Cinders and embers flew over them. Krystal turned. She glanced up. The firelight cast its glow upon her scarred face, shining what should have been the mask of its fury, strangely glowing a violent cleansing corona, so that Maishe saw only the original smooth flesh and how incredibly beautiful she had been destined to be.

"Holy Mother of God, Maishe. The fire. I can feel the fire all over, all over again."

"Krystal, we have to rescue Julia."

"So soon? I want to be one with the fire now. I need, I must be one with."

"No. Now. Come! Obey me at once."

"Yes, Maishe. For you." And, once freed from her bonds, the naked sacrificial creature sprang into their arms and he held them both for a long time while the fire advanced about them, destroying the evil, washing it away, cleansing it. Only then did it begin gradually to ebb, then to die.

"Maishe."

"Yes, Krystal."

"Can we go to California now?"

"Yes, Krystal."

And Maishe Rosstein knew he had accomplished something in his life, after all.

Then, in their final heaving torment lashing into nothingness, he thought he heard the fire flames snicker.

The Mountains

7

Rock

It was when Maishe emerged from the enclosed darkness of the Eisenhower Tunnel and regained the peculiar angle of the mountain light that he knew he could, at last, leave Hyacinth behind him. He had regretted leaving but, he had long ago made a vow to Krystal he knew he could not take back. As for Julia, she went wherever they went. Actually, Maishe knew now that Julia went wherever Krystal went. He now had no doubt she loved Krystal more than him, and that was the real reason she came along, He felt neither remorse, nor judgment, nor jealousy. He had always felt like a protecting father to them both.

Although the women were not that far apart in age, Krystal was clearly the mom, Julia the daughter. Or, at times, something else, something strange, almost unspeakable, and, at the same time, something beautiful. It had been like that from the beginning, from the moment Julia entered their car, scarred and rain-soaked and scared. Maishe suddenly realized that he seemed to be attracted to and attracted scarred, scared women. Maybe it was because he understands them better than anyone else. He too, harbored deep scars and fears.

At that moment, as he egressed the tunnel, emerging from darkness into light, he envisioned a vision that he would become, in the time of his old age, a comfortable grandfather to their children.

The mountains wore a sprinkle of green from their early spring. In the lowlands lush greenery and roadside purple wildflowers showed already early hints of summer; but up here winter lingered, her snowcaps still visible on the tops of peaks all about them. He had never seen so many large eagles, playing the updrafts of the lakes and valleys, their wings spread wide to reveal ebony and white-tipped feather-fingers at the ends.

He had heard the endangered species laws were working and the magnificent birds, flying high and flying far, masters of the mountain ranges, had, in recent years, increased in numbers. An occasional deer-like animal bounded through the trees below the tree-line, in the deeper-set regions. All about him glories rose then hid behind greater peaks or lesser peaks at the distance. Still, they climbed, up, ever up; it seemed all the Acclaim could do to hold its own against the grade.

"My God, Maishe, it's beautiful," Julia said. For an instant, she sounded like Krystal. Increasingly, she was taking on Krystal's mannerisms and voice patterns. But Krystal was a good mimic as well, he had noticed. Perhaps they could both be actresses when they got to California. Yes, and he could manage them both. Or he'd find a good manager for them; yes, that was it; then, as the years passed, and they waxed successful, the girls would take care of him. Indeed, in the wealth of his old age, he could sit out behind the house by the beach and watch the waves wash in, caressing the smooth sand, and watch the waves wash out, teasing the minute water-molded dunes along the shoreline, while the women cared for him, looked after him, tended him, and he played with the children of these two women and told the kids stories true, stories exaggerated, and stories made up. It was his vision and his vision quest; he knew it would come to pass, just as he envisioned it.

"It's magnificent, Maishe," Krystal said.

He missed the Vega. He missed it a great deal. He missed it like a man misses a woman he has known in his youth, when sex and love were strange partners and the bodies of women astonished him in their infinite varieties, skin markings, softness of flesh, responses.

Maishe had always adored women, worshipped them actually, their hair, their eyes (my God, their eyes), their slim fingers, the way they talked and moved. And he missed the lime-neon green Vega that way, with a feeling of emptiness and sorrow, not just in his heart, but in all the nerve endings of his flesh and muscle.

As he had feared, the frame had rusted out from underneath. The beautiful tapered body, the long graceful design, had separated from the very skeleton of the car. Like most Chevrolets he knew, the engine could probably run on down the road forever. They had let him take over the payments on the Acclaim and he had agreed to supply part of the down payment on a new car. Now as they strained up the grades, Corvettes, Cadillacs, Mercedes passed them as though they stood still. Still, they trudged on, each growing silent for a while, awed by the majesty and the glory of the infinite Rocky Mountain Range, the passengers of the car haunted by their memories, the mountains harboring great mysteries and secrets. They passed old mining towns, some of the mines clearly working yet today. They passed through newer towns, as night approached on a lonely Rocky Mountain highway, heading west. Occasionally they stopped. Then they headed on again.

Finally, the road leveled out for a spell. The temperature gauge on the Acclaim crept down to a normal scale. Maishe had grown concerned as the red needle approached the higher bar. Soon, at dusk, the lights of a larger town, or a series of villages, twinkled like starlight against a deepening cosmic truth. The road signs announced they had arrived at Vale. It was about halfway through the mountain passes. They decided to put in for the night.

"Well, girls, I'll buy you a decent meal tonight. Vale is known for its skiing, its mountain views, its shopping, its fine restaurants, and something else."

What? They fairly chimed in. Like a chorus of angels, Maishe thought.

"Beautiful women. But then, I'm the one bringing in a car to upset the balance even more."

"Oh, Maishe."

They fairly chimed together. Then he heard a sound he hadn't heard since the terrible night of fire and death, of betrayal and loyalty. He heard them giggle, the giggle of happy girls. And Maishe Rosstein knew the healing had begun. They went to the southern part of Vale, the part that was to their left, for the freeway split the town in two. They drove through the clean, curving shopping mall—like streets for a while, until they found the hotel they wanted, the one at the foot of the mountain, Vale Manor. When Maishe got out of the car, he was surprised to find he felt a chill in the air. The girls were happy and giggly again, as young women should be from time to time, but he suddenly felt as though someone had walked on his grave.

He let the women unload as he looked up the majestic rise of the mountain and glanced at the boardwalk pathways to his left. He felt, not for the first time, but stronger now, that someone was following them. He shivered. He entered the building. The strong breeze that had come up died down. Krystal returned to the car, to retrieve more baggage. She stopped, suddenly, almost as an animal in the woods stopped to sniff the air. To her surprise, she realized they weren't more than a quarter-mile off the freeway. One could hear the whines of the engines. Suddenly she shivered. At once she didn't feel safe. She didn't know why. She collected all the bags at once. Loaded down, she ran as best she could inside to be with Maishe.

******

The rooms sang to them. As soon as they entered, they scurried through the apartment, looking at and touching the convenience kitchens, the well-appointed and space-filled living rooms, two full-size bedrooms, and two full baths. They were more like residence apartments than hotel rooms. Since they had known each other, loved each other, solved cases together, studied together, it was the best they had known. The rooms were more luxurious than they dreamed or hoped. They decided to stay awhile, perhaps through some of the summer. Maishe knew they needed to leave enough time to make it through the north rim before the first snow. They had agreed to visit the Canyon before heading on to Vegas and L.A. with the money he had found at the site of terror, the part of their salaries they had saved, and the small separation bonus the county had scrapped together out of gratitude, he felt they had enough to stay, get to L.A., and have a small nest egg for a good start.

By any stretch they could not stay up here a long time; but a few days or a couple of weeks, if they were careful the rest of the way, wouldn't put too much of a crimp in their budget. They'd have to be especially careful in Las Vegas, he knew, although he still considered himself a good poker player. He'd probably win a little. He knew, he certainly wouldn't lose very much. Maishe played his cards right, generally investing only in the more probable winning hands. He played the kind of game the house did not like to see played.

No, they could stay a while, hike through the woods, climb halfway up the mountain, stroll through the town and shops, sleep late, take the mountain air. Already he could feel his sinuses improving. He was now a long way from Omaha, even farther distant from Louisville, his old home town. Then, inexplicably, he fell into one of those terrible pits of depression. For he realized fully, completely, like most men realize sooner or later, that he would have done better for himself staying in his home town and building his life upon the building of those who had come before him.

It was summer elsewhere, but it was still spring in the mountains, and he felt cold again, not just by the cool night air. Vale was a bit too plastic, a bit too much like a plastic picture postcard, the ones with the description on the top of the left half of the back of the picture, with the address space to the right, and the space for the stamp in the top right corner of the address half. One never knew how much the denomination of the stamp to lick and squash on the little square space. Still, the village was easy to like, the mountains were the mountains, their rooms were gorgeous, comfortable, the girls were generous, and he felt privileged to be needed by them and to need them.

Nonetheless, he couldn't shake his growing edginess, his inevitable uneasiness. He thought, then, of his wife and daughter and how he should have done things differently. He'd call Natalie and ask her to come spend a few days with him.

It was a beautiful location. They could be reunited, become a father and a daughter again. It evolved into an idyllic time. In the morning, they slept in. The sun crept in through mountain passes to the east. The light diffused against the beige curtain. Maishe liked to get up, occasionally pleased to discover a morning erection, pad to the bathroom, return to watch the girls, innocent in their sleep. The deep sleep of the young and young-at-heart. It was amazing how beautiful Krystal looked at those times, as if her flesh was reborn anew at night, then, as the day wore on, it stretched into the multi-patch fabric which fascinated and reviled at the same time. With Julia's mouth open, Maishe always liked to inspect the caps on her teeth he had spent so much money on. She was odd, Julia. She had said nothing about that night since it happened, but he noticed she too no longer liked fires. In fact, Maishe and Krystal observed at last that the matches had disappeared from their luggage and other possessions. Krystal, on the other hand, had seemed to lose her pyrophobia. In fact, she now seemed almost pyromaniacal, fascinated with every flicker of flame.

He liked to go back to bed against the morning gray light, to doze thinking how his life might have been so different. To doze, thinking, to dream, wondering, like an old man—or a young one. The afternoon, while it was warm, they splashed in the pool. Toward evening, they hiked up the mountainside. At night, they meandered through the village streets, stopping to listen to the street musicians, dining at one of the fine restaurants. Natalie came. She stayed for a few days. Maishe was astonished at how famously his three women hit it off. They resurrected their friendship. They looked forward to the time they would see each other again. They giggled like schoolgirls. They shopped like women. They dined lunch in restaurants like wealthy matrons.

During those times, the girls went off on their own, he wandered about the trails. Alternately, he felt old and young within hours, sometimes within minutes. Occasionally, his prostatitis and his vasitis flared up and he took to his bed, with aspirin and ice packs, while the girls went shopping or just walking about. Once they came back ebullient, having taken the tram to the top of the head snow-trail mountain. Truly it must be a sight in the wintertime, the ski-trails etched across the glistening velvet whiteness, like that scene in the Hitchcock movie with Gregory Peck and Ingrid Bergman, where Peck succumbed to a fugue and believed he was the psychiatrist rather than the patient that needed help, treatment; of course, Bergman, a talented psychiatrist and faithful lover believed in her charge and brought him back from the chasm, on the ski-slope mountain. Somehow he didn't feel jealous of the people who pursued that strange sport. He knew he'd rather be chasing some bad guys, shoving an evil thug's face into the car door a little too hard.

He knew then why he felt the emptiness, the loss. He missed it. He missed the action. He missed rockin' and rollin'. He missed the early morning walks when the night and the county were his alone. He missed the juice, as the cops say. When his daughter left, she gave all three of them a large hug, pregnant with love. He knew then how much he missed Natasha, a beautiful, intelligent, talented, lovely daughter of his.

For the first time, he realized she hadn't asked about his wife, her mother. Her grades were good and she was thinking of being a doctor. He promised he'd try to help her any way he could. In this languid fashion, the days passed. As usual, he felt more at home at night. He always felt that the night enveloped him like a warm woman friend, welcoming him in her comforting bosom while overhead the star-sparkles of her eyes shined and glistened a hundred thousand glows and glimmers of mystery and trust. The streets with their horse-drawn cabs, the street musicians, the crowds walking and talking as in a mall, the tiered homes, and townhouses up on the hillsides, their lights glimmering an affluent warmth of sultry satisfaction and accomplishment within—it all took him to an indefinable place where, for a short time, he felt at one, at peace with the universe. For a time in the night's early hours, as usual, the melancholy lifted.

The sense of great loss washed over him, the worst of it in the afternoon. In the afternoon, the oppressive blackness of daylight captured him. He felt himself spinning deep through a vortex, down into a spiral-etched pit. He tried to keep from reaching the bottom, for he was not sure if this time he would be able to climb out, with or without help. The girls worried, for he was not like himself, not like their Maishe.

One day, they walked across the wooden bridge, oblique to the parking lot. It delved into a small wooded glade. They had been meaning to do it for some time. Always, the mountain and the village had beckoned. But this afternoon, they found themselves outside. They took to the trail. This was the highest point of the tree line, Maishe reckoned. He told Julia and Krystal. As usual, they appreciated the knowledge. *Well,* thought Maishe, *how did Shirley Maclaine put it: You can take the girl out of the chorus line but you can't take the chorus line out of the girl.* So—here he was—proving a paraphrase for another profession—you can take the teacher out of the classroom but you can't take the classroom out of the teacher.

He lectured. They listened. They absorbed material, their minds like sponges. Like their youthful bodies aching with insatiable lust, he could never give their yearning minds all they needed. The bridge crossed a creek, a clean, fresh mountain stream. Clearly, it was as pure and clean as it was at its source, not far away. Already it moved quick, eddying and whipping foams and sprays of water over and about rocks and sticks in its watery way. Plumes of fan-shaped droplets leaped to the bottom of the wooden walk-span.

For a long while, they gazed over both sides of the bridge. They listened to the bubbles, gurgles, gee-gaws of clean running water. They played the stick game that Poo and Tigger and Robin played, throwing the stick in the upstream side of the water, running the few steps to the other side to see their sticks emerge from under the bridge. They raced the sticks, then argued over who had won.

A few other guests crossed the bridge and threw them strange stares. The girls covered their mouths, opened their eyes wide, and giggled. The fire of not so long ago suddenly seemed far away, washed in the true water of the earth coursing beneath them. They walked. Soon they emerged into a large clearing. There were signs directing them to an amphitheater or a playground. As it turned out, they had to walk through the playing fields to get to the amphitheater.

Some girls played volleyball. The man and the two women stopped for a while to watch. The teams shouted. The teams screamed. Both teams applauded, it seemed to him, whether one team won the point or not. Apparently, if one lost a point, the team tried to buck itself up for the next one. It was a wonderful thing about sports; within a set time, a victor and a defeated emerged, and it was over until the next set time.

Woody Allen's line, concerning the unreality of movies, came to him: "If only life…could be like this."

An injury occurred. One girl kicked another under the net. She went down. She was unable to return. Maishe started to go over to see if he could help. But she limped away, with another girl helping her. It didn't seem serious. The teams were a player short. Julia leaped at the chance. Maishe and Krystal watched from the side, feeling the pride parents feel as they look on while their athlete-child performs well at the game. And Julia, surprisingly, had clearly played the game before. Maishe put his arm about his wife-surrogate, mother-surrogate, and they commented with shared pride to each other how well their temporary surrogate daughter was doing.

Soon it was over. She skipped-returned to them, with the flush and deep-set clear-featured eyes of the returning athlete who has made a contribution in the game. They made their way about the twisting path to the amphitheater. The gates and the box office windows were closed. There were advertisements, however, broadsides. Maishe was impressed to see Tammy Wynette and Mel Tillis were coming toward the end of summer. They wouldn't see them. By then, they would be gone, somewhere out on the desert heading west to Los Angeles.

They peered through the closed gates for a while, trying to get an idea of the layout. But it was too difficult. There was a wall within that twisted and turned and blocked their view. They made their way along the other side and came to a natural rock pool with a small waterfall.

"This might be the very spring with began the creek," Maishe mused.

"The creek's too big, too close," Krystal said. "This is just a small tributary."

Maishe knew she was right. Julia nodded. She hopped up and down over the pool. She was still feeling athletic, flush and energetic with the victory her team had enjoyed. They sat down. They watched the water cascading over the rocks. The falls dropped small, calm, gently, but with that comforting burbling water sound. There were some fish in the pool, small redfish, when they saw the people, the fish darted and dashed about, trying to find hiding places deep in the lower crevices of the rocks.

After a while, Maishe said, "I once was accepted to film school. I never went."

"What," Krystal said. "Why on earth not?"

"I don't know," Maishe said. "After all these years, I never figured out why, although recently I've been thinking that it wasn't because I didn't have it in me; it was because I had a sense of duty, an obligation to my family at the time. But look at me now, heading out west on a trip, I should have taken a quarter-century ago. Still, after all these years, I always regretted I didn't go. Funny, isn't it? We regret more what we did not do, rather than what we did, even if it was an erroneous thing. All those years. My life sure would have been different—maybe better, maybe worse—but certainly different and without a major regret."

"It's time to go, isn't it?" Julia said.

"Yes. We leave tomorrow," Maishe said, suddenly realizing he had made the decision just as she spoke.

Krystal smiled. She hugged her knees to her chin, with her arms around them. She rocked ever so gently, to and fro, as she did sometimes.

"Damn," Julia said. "Just when I find some volleyballers to play with."

******

They found themselves stuck on Interstate 70. They were coming down, heading out of the mountains' western side. There had been a bad wreck. Men and women in orange and yellow helmets and coveralls, their hands thick with gravel, dust, and blood scurried like ants in and about an immense open land-scarred man-made anthill.

Bulldozers, caterpillars, backhoes, grade plows plied their rumbling way along the hills and paths of the giant series of roads and small dirt-filled mountains.

Gravel and dust filled the air. Emergency workers tried to get to the wrecked cars, tried to get the cars unhinged in the midst of the construction site. The mountain pass was a tricky narrow grade. Even Maishe could see the workers were allowed no room for error. Both lanes westbound had to be closed. They soon came down from 65 miles per hour to a dead stop. Long twisting lanes of metal, plastic, and chrome wound out like played wire strands before them and forming aft.

"It's still morning. Let's have a second cup of coffee. Let's read the paper," Krystal said.

She took out the new Thermos they had purchased in Vale. They wanted to buy something before they left. Julia had found this large Thermos at a close-out sale. It had three cups stacked over the top of the grey, beige, and green striped cylinder. The large twist-cap was red. The three cups were red, green, and gray. Maishe's spirits had been lifted a bit since his daughter's visit. Green had always been one of his favorite colors. He liked pink, too. Maishe took the green cup. He was not surprised when Krystal took the red cup.

She held it between both her hands, like a geisha must do in the tea ceremony, he thought. She held it up. She looked underneath it. She inspected both sides. She fondled the cup with her long, tapering, feminine fingers free of scars. She always did that. Then she sipped slowly, her gems of sparkling eyes peering over the rim.

Julia took the grey. She was happy because it was the largest of the three, the bottom one, around which the other two ringed shut, locked in place. Julia held her cup with one hand. With the other hand, she held her section of the paper. She blew steam off the top of the still-hot liquid. The cups had twirls and whorls inside, near the top. The whorls and twirls allowed the cups to be screwed tight, one seated on top of the other, gentle, firm, secure, smooth.

The Thermos worked well. It kept hot things hot. It kept cold things cold. They all liked the Thermos. They were glad Julia had found it. They were glad she had bought it. They were glad to be together, making something out of a morning of being stuck in a nightmare of a traffic jam. Occasionally, Julia put her section of the paper down. She whisked the lock of reddish-brown-blonde hair that always fell down over her forehead and never stayed long where she whisked it.

Drinking coffee, relaxing, reading the morning paper in a traffic jam on the freeway. *Really,* Maishe thought, *they should do well in California after all.* The endless line of chrome, metal, plastic began to move, creeping at first, starting, stopping, crawling. Only one lane seemed open. The cars in the unfortunate lane of wrong choice tried to get over. Their signal lights blinked incessantly. Slowly they advanced. Julia looked up, stretched, and gazed all about her.

"Oh my god," she said.

It was an edge in her voice he hadn't heard since that night.

"What is it, babe," Krystal said.

"Julia?" Maishe said.

"He's, he's out there. He's following us. I know it."

"Who?"

"Him. Junior. I saw his face."

"Oh, shit," Krystal said.

"Where, Julia?" Maishe said.

"There—damn, I don't see him now. A truck's moved in front. He was there. Back there. A half-mile or so behind us. I know it. I just…"

They could not see any sign of the monster again. They drove on. Soon, they were past the tie-up. He was able to open the car up, He noticed he was speeding. He didn't slow down. Krystal shivered. He noticed he did not stop to comfort her.

"Damn," Julia said. "This coffee's gone cold and I spilled it anyway."

Maishe Rosstein drove on, down, out of the mountains.

******

It was still day. He drove on. On and on. The land was flat now. It began to look like Monument Valley in all those old John Wayne movies. It seemed the ribbon of the road stretched endlessly before him, a four land divided highway with no access roads, just two divided sets of two black lines between endless vistas of sagebrush and an occasional hillock or small solitary mountain. Fences snaked along the border of the freeway. Off in the distance, single-lane dirt and gravel roads slithered through this strange near-desert.

They reminded him of the Iowa and Nebraska farm access roads visible off their main highways, with their fences snaking and slithering along their roads. Here, he suspected, spread out no mere farms of a paltry 160 or 320 acres. No doubt huge ranches, as large as many townships in the east and midwest, lay somewhere out there, in the middle of nowhere, the house and the other buildings of the compound far in the hinterlands.

He noticed buzzards circling in the distance, biding their time over some unfortunate creature. No doubt it had been stalked, hunted by another creature, then brought to its end in a last desperate gasp of a struggle. More than usual, he glanced up to the mirror. Few cars traversed the bareness of southern Utah. In fact, for twenty miles now, he'd only counted five on either side of the highway. Occasionally, though, in the mirror, he caught a glimpse of a moving blue dot just visible before the horizon. He noticed Julia and Krystal also looked back over their shoulders. They sat in silence. He felt their tension permeating through the car. He drove. On and on he drove.

He was glad he had stopped the car when they came out of the mountains. Here only sagebrush and rock, sand and tumbleweeds greeted them from either side as they rode; these, and far-flung hills which seemed to move along with them. They had driven thirty miles out of Colorado. They had sixty more to go to the next exit. At the speed he was speeding, he knew he could close it in forty minutes.

He tried, again and again, to go over it and over it in his mind. Could that hulking creep have escaped the battle unharmed? Had he been able to run, crawl, skulk out of the ring of fire and exploding barn? Had he his escape route planned? Maishe didn't think he was that smart. It was probably pure dumb luck—Maishe's, Julia's, Krystal's dumb luck. *Of course, she could be wrong. It may have been someone who looked like him, that's all. Just another innocent sap, trapped by poor planning and poor road design, like them. That could be all it was,* Maishe thought. *In fact, that must be it.*

"I'll kill him," Julia said.

It was the first thing any of them had said since they stopped for gas and checked the map, looking furtively about them the whole time. "I swear it. I'll kill him. I mean it. I'll get a gun somehow and I'll shoot him dead. I'll shoot and I'll shoot. I'll kill him,"

Maishe drove on. The buzzards in the distance circled lower. The large hill-mountain south of them moved along with them. Tumbleweeds stacked against the fences to their right.

"Maishe?"

"Yes, Julia."

"I wish I was playing volleyball."

"I know."

Tension rode along in the car. And silence again. He drove to the exit which was the first exit ninety miles out of Colorado.

******

For a moment he thought, he hadn't found it yet, it was just two trailers, two mobile homes, set on either side of the road. The road curved up quickly, went to sand and gravel, curled about, and stopped. One trailer had an old 50s style gas pump in front of it, the kind with a small lit logo circle top that men in bow ties, crisp uniforms, and clean rags would stand around on the old Milton Berle Show. It was the Texaco Hour and any week the men in crisp ties and uniforms opened the show by singing a song.

We are the men from Texaco,
We something, something Maine to Mexico,
We never something always get it right
Something, something…

Maishe felt sad, suddenly, and alone. He couldn't remember the song. Krystal and Julia probably wouldn't even know who Milton Berle was. His wife would know. In fact, she would probably remember the song.

"We are the men fr…"

It was no use. He could not remember. Maishe liked the Milton Berle Show. Uncle Miltie, he was called. He didn't recall many specific bits. There was Sam, the assistant. Her name was Samantha, but the running gag was that Uncle Miltie called out, "Sam" and this breathless blonde ditz appeared. Except (he was fuzzy on this point) it seemed she always got the last laugh somehow. He couldn't recall much else; but he remembered he liked it. Years later he read Milton Berle's biography. He was surprised to read that no matter how long the comedian had been on, he was depressed and distraught when his show was canceled.

There was an entry in the autobiography that Buick had sponsored the show the last few years, or was it Oldsmobile? Maishe only remembered the Texaco men. He didn't recall the Buick commercials. Maishe recalled other programs he liked from that time. The Jack Benny Program. Dragnet. Rawhide. Gunsmoke. Wagon Train. Somehow it seemed T.V. shows were better then. In fact, he knew that they even showed some of the later Gunsmokes; and he preferred them to the more recent travesties television had dallied with.

This pump had no Texaco men about it. It had only a Mexican name he didn't recognize. Out of Texas and Oklahoma, it said. He had to read it twice for it said $5.00 a gallon, and below, 82 octane. He parked the car. They scurried out. They looked down toward the freeway for a while and about them. They went up to the trailer that served as a store. Across the way, at the other trailer, some cowboys bent over the open engine of a pick-up truck, occasionally laughing or shouting a whoop. To the left of the store, a girl about five or six was trying to draw water out of a hole in the ground.

"Spring's dry now Elsa. Gotta wait till dark. It'll come up past nightfall. Always does."

The woman who shouted out the door was one of those big-boned women who looked like she should have been fat, but whose legs looked trim and fit in shorts and mini-skirts. She had a strange asymmetrical quality to her face. She was one of those women who at once excited all men and other women could never figure out why. To their right side, a cowboy stood leaning with his back against the wall, one booted foot on the ground, the left up behind him on the wall. He guzzled a bottle of cold Rocky Road beer, then, holding it at the nape of the bottle with long callused dirt-streaked fingers, dangled it by his side.

Occasionally he lifted his Stetson and shouted, to the men across the way, "Hey Pete. Pete. Ol' Pete." Maishe glanced out across the way. If Ol' Pete was in the group working on the truck, he wasn't looking up or he was "deaf."

On the other side of the door, a girl with long, curly red hair sat on her duffel bag. She looked at Julia and Krystal as they came by. Soon the women were talking. Maishe ambled up to the big woman, clearly, the owner of this entire complex, such as it was. No doubt that was her truck, as well. Some other rusted trucks and cars, at random angles of repose, rested behind the home, Maishe now saw.

"Elsa. Leave the hose alone. Spring'll come up tonight. Or tomorrow morning toward dawn."

"Pete. Hey 'Ol Pete," the cowboy shouted.

"Shut up Hank," the woman said.

She wore a tank top. The high mounds of her breasts spilled over it. When she shouted or when she walked or when she ran, Maishe noticed her mounds quivered. He stared at them whenever they quivered. He tried to avert his eyes just before she looked at him. Her bare arms were big but muscular. When she moved them, they did not quiver. She looked great in the tight red shorts.

"Shiet," Hank said. He gulped another swing of beer. The liquid in the bottle jostled. The men across the way whooped.

"Found it," Hank said.

"Hey, Ol Pete," he shouted.

"Shut up, damn it. I said shut up and get away."

"Shiet."

"Howdy," Maishe said. He didn't mean to say "Howdy."

He meant to say, "Hi," "Howdy" came out. He saw a small sign above the roof: Mary Ellen's. It was one of those signs the Coca-Cola Company made, half their logo, the other half the local privately owned small business's sign.

"Yea," the woman said.

"You must be Mary Ellen."

The three young women in front laughed at something they said. Mary Ellen shouted at Elsa again. The child kept poking the green garden hose down the hole, like one of those intelligent tool-making chimpanzees Jane Goodall found that poke termite hills with specially designed sticks, skillfully knowing where the hidden doorways of the nests lie. It was a skill Goodall, a human being, had never been able to duplicate nor to discern. The chimpanzees then eat the termites off their specially designed poke-sticks.

"She'll get stuck by that ol' scorpion. Serves her right."

"You'll get stung by Mr. Scorpion, Elsa," Mary Ellen shouted.

"Pete. Hey 'Ol Pete," Hank shouted.

"Shut up, Hank," Mary Ellen shouted. Then, to Maishe, "What do you want?"

"Well, excuse me, but, that is—well, I mean to say—$5.00 a gallon—and for 82 octane?"

"Go to the next stinking hole, then. It's only 120 miles west and hotter and lonelier than this godforsaken place. I can make it $10.00 a gallon if'n I like. Hell, $15. $20. In a minute, I think I will."

"Ah. Well, ma'am, no offense intended. That is to say, $5.00 will be fine."

Suddenly, Maishe was surprised to see Mary Ellen walk to the pump and service his car. She walked with a fluid strength, a power, he noticed. Still, there was something about her that seemed tired, used. The men across the way whooped it up. The three women by the store laughed.

"Shut up, Hank," Mary Ellen shouted.

"I didn't say shiet," Hank said. "Shiet."

He lifted the bottle. He killed it. Maishe noticed Mary Ellen had given up on pulling Elsa away from the spring hole. His women and the other girl walked toward him.

"Fill up?" Mary Ellen shouted.

"Yes," Maishe shouted.

"Maishe," Krystal said. "This here is Elana. She's a masseuse. She needs to go to a job in Vegas. We're going through Vegas, aren't we? I mean, we planned to stay a few days there, right?"

He didn't want to take another mouth to feed but he knew he could never refuse Krystal anything. A tumbleweed, a large one, floated by, hitting his car, then skimmed the land toward where the men still bent over the open hood. The ball of dead grasses hit one of the men. He kicked it with his boot without looking up. The tumbleweed continued on out into the desert, no doubt to come up against a fence off the freeway. Maishe managed to hear most of what the tumbleweed said as it passed him by.

"Well, Maishe," the tumbleweed said. "You've got another mouth to feed. Seems I heard tell that happened to you once before."

"Hey, 'Ol Pete," Hank shouted.

"Shit," Mary Ellen said. She said that to no one. She said that to the large lonely sky and to the shy lonesome rock, to the isolated eroded hills, to the tumbling tumbleweeds that bounced across the land endlessly like a defeated returning ragtag remnant of an army.

Then she said to Maishe, "Looks like you're taking on passengers."

"Looks like it." Maishe suddenly knew the story in advance. He looked her over for the dozenth time, the way a man of any age does when he sees a woman he knows is full of sex.

"Well, I'm ready too. I've had it. Look at my hair. Strings. Ropes. Catguts. Dried out. It was ash-blonde once. Now it's just ash. What do you say? And the gas is on me."

Maishe looked at the pump. It read 14 gallons, $70.

"What about the girl? The store? The truck? Hank? Pete?"

"Hey, Hank," Mary Ellen shouted. "Place's your'n now.

"Watch Elsa till Loren comes back toward nightfall. If'n you don't keep her away from that scorpion, I'll come back and I'll bust both your arms and crush your nuts like a busted bull's balls."

"Shiet," Hank said.

"I'll get my stuff. Clean out my cash register too, all $177 of it."

Soon she returned, carrying a large duffel bag. Maishe knew he could probably barely lift off the ground. She carried it like a hulking marine lifts his gear, as if it were a feather, with one arm. He opened the trunk. She threw in her gear. She picked up Elana's gear like the bags were empty.

"It's a sign," Mary Ellen said.

"What?" Elana said.

"It's a sign. I was standing by the spring-hole this morning. I looked up and one small white fluffy cloud floated by. In all this aching loneliness, one little white-grey cloud hovered over the spring. *Must be God's own puff of joy*, I thought."

"I'm a Scorpio," Elana said. "We're intellectual, you know." The girl had large round eyes, blue, like the lonesome sky.

Mary Ellen continued, "I said, out loud I said it, oh, Lord God, You come even here to see your devoted doting daughter. Now let it be that this day if your messenger-man comes out of the desert and so says unto me that the price of my pump-gas be too high, but complains not after I say so, and he says then oh Lord of Mercy such that he be listening to your heavenly words, to fill up his tank, that that be your messenger-man I leave with and go on wherever on your own world he be going.

"That is what I said early this morning as the light come on out of the lonesome sky. And then you come on. And you said the words. And in the beginning, there was the word. And it's a sign. And we're going, ain't we?"

"Aren't we," Maishe said.

"Maishe is an English professor," Krystal said. "Sort of."

"Maishe knows a lot of things," Julia said.

"I'm a masseuse," Elana said. "I want to start a practice in Vegas."

"A sign from God. I knew Maishe and Krystal were—I just knew," Julia said.

"An English teacher, eh?"

"Well, a police officer these days. Retired I guess," Maishe said.

"Maishe saved our lives," Julia said. "He's a messenger from God."

"Yea, so he is," Mary Ellen said. "What kind of name is Maishe, anyway?"

"One given to me by God."

"Yea."

"Let's go," Krystal said.

"I'm ready," Elana said.

"Listen," Maishe said.

"What?"

"Did you hear the tumbleweed say anything?"

"No," they said, in concert, albeit not in unison.

"I didn't either. Strange."

"Tumbleweeds don't normally say nothing," Mary Ellen said.

"They got silent minds, like the desert. Sometimes, at night, though, they whistlin' and groanin'. Groanin' something fierce, at night sometimes, just before the dawn."

"Let's go," Krystal said.

"I'm ready," Elana said.

They piled in. For the first time, Julia sat upfront with Maishe and Krystal. The large woman and the woman with great spewing curly red hair, an infectious guffaw-laden laugh, and with radish-glowing freckles on her shoulders got in the back.

Maishe liked freckles on women, especially brown-red freckles on reddish-skin on red-headed women. Elana's cascades of frothy red curls flowed about her, framing her bright, burnt orange lipstick and her glossy lapis lazuli eyes. Like Julia, she always tried to coerce an errant curl back in place, to no avail. Julia's errant tresses fell straight, however, like the rest of her long brown hair. Maishe began to pull out onto the gravel road leading back to the interstate, about a quarter-mile away.

"Son of a bitch," Mary Ellen said.

Maishe stopped the car.

"What is it?" Julia said.

"Look at that," Mary Ellen said.

"What," Elana said.

"First time that fucking spring even come up with the daylight. And I never have seen it froth like that. Never. Like God's own garden-creation spring water." Of a sudden, a great spewing froth caromed out of the hole. The child sat back on the ground, laughing and clapping her hands. Maishe's view was over Elana's shoulder. He was struck by the cascading flow of the water and foam matching the pattern of Elana's scarlet-tressed cascades. He was also reminded of those lawn sprinklers in suburban neighborhoods which tilted first one way, then slowly, inexorably, in the other direction, the pattern of their flow intact, consistent.

"Damn," Krystal said.

"Awesome," Julia said. "I almost forgot about my teeth-caps."

"God Almighty," Mary Ellen said.

Hank ran with a bucket to the spring. The other men from across the yard ran and tramped over with their buckets. The child sat, then stood, then hopped gleefully wet, up and down, dancing and jumping in and out of the water. All the occupants of the car watched the unabated flowing forth of the sparkling clean pirouetting waters. Finally, Krystal turned. She sat forward.

"Let's go, Maishe," she said. It was a voice and an attitude that had grown in her since he'd known her. Suddenly, he remembered they'd better go, although he had to admit that with Mary Ellen now along, he felt a little more secure. He felt for the .38 he always carried now. As always it was there in the small of his back.

He rumbled out, the car shaking and jostling on the ill-maintained road. Krystal looked straight ahead, occasionally glaring about. The other women looked back over their shoulders out the back of the car. The child danced and screeched with delight, showering in the water. The men held their buckets out, capturing the returning waterfall of spray and droplets. Just before they lost sight of it, as fast and sudden as it had come up, it stopped.

"Damn," Elana said.

"Here's the turn, Maishe," Krystal said.

"I know," Maishe said, an edge to his voice he hadn't meant to put there.

"I didn't mean—shit," Krystal said.

"Where we headed?" Mary Ellen said.

Maishe looked over at Krystal. She sulked. Those gorgeous blue eyes sunk deeper set into her face-mask than ever. He hated it when she went deep inside herself like that. *What was wrong now? Now why did she sulk?* He thought he knew only part of it. For the rest, like all women really, she would always remain a mystery to him.

"California," Maishe said.

"I'm going to Vegas," Elana said. "I've got a job waiting for me. Supposed to be, anyway."

"Right on. Maybe I can see the ocean."

"I'm driving straight to the edge of it," Maishe said. "Straight to the edge of water and shore."

Krystal shifted in her seat. She sighed. Julia yawned. It was a long yawn, stretched and sad. She said she was tired. She leaned against Krystal's shoulder. Krystal softened a bit.

She circled her arm around Julia. She held her.

"California. Yea. The ocean. That's good enough," Mary Ellen said. "I have never seen the ocean."

Maishe said something under his breath; even he wasn't sure what it was.

"You can stretch your legs out over me, if you like, woman of the water," Elana said. "I don't mind."

Maishe heard rustling from the back. Soon he heard Mary Ellen murmur, "Hmm, that feels good."

"I'm a masseuse," Elana said.

"That feels real good. Mmmm. Yea."

Maishe drove on through the endless western afternoon, on the endless ribbon of road. The tumbleweeds piled against the fences to his right. The sun glinted off the rare car on the other side. The hill mountain to his left followed him along. Just before dusk, he noticed the buzzards began to swoop down.

Later, he drove through the dusk south on a two-lane, winding road. He had finally found the turn-off. It had been a long ride, and a long ride was to come. He was sure there would be no place to stop until the canyon, and the map gave no indication the road would be an easy one. In fact, it looked mountainous and full of curves and he would be tackling it at night. The women were coming about, for the most part, coming awake with the onset of dusk, those in the front seat at least.

The two in the back seat hadn't really stopped what they were doing since they first loaded the car and each other. *Well, what was the difference, after all*, Maishe thought. Everyone on the planet had to live. The alternative for most of us was too much.

So that was the answer, so simple, a received text, the clear answer to all the eternal questions, granted in God's own back yard, on a pristine day and a bright red sunset dusk out in one of the few environments that had not been ruined, against it a man and four women, hurtling through the rocks, gradually appearing cliffs, natural and manmade gullies, these stones and hills laid down as it had been hundreds of thousands of years ago--the ancient stones called out the eternal answer to him—just let everybody do as they wished so long as they didn't harm another person.

Maishe had always adored women. Now here he was, out in the southwestern desert, responsible for four. They had a long way to go. Already they ate him up alive with their moods, their demands. It was the way with women. That's how they were, that was all, and he was here, the appointed one, to take care of them; he had to tolerate and consider their needs, individual and in concert.

He drove on through the night that gained upon them suddenly. Just as suddenly small towns appeared. He passed through. He wondered what motivated someone to live in a town or village out where even the buzzards don't fly over. He was in Navaho country now. The signs welcomed him to the nation. Mountains leaped like horned dear, at odd angles. Valleys and deep gorges plunged beneath the earth.

Risen and gashed, gashed and risen, it appeared the lands had allowed an ancient benevolent tormentor to extrude stone, to chip away at rock for all eternity.

"How much further, Maishe?" Krystal said. For a moment he sat startled. It was the first time she had said something since they left the gas station.

"About five hours, maybe, with some luck. The mountains and gorges have begun. This is an astonishing country. If the moon climbs higher you can see some amazing formations."

"I'm hungry," Julia said.

"I can't help it. There is nothing between here and there," Maishe snapped. He had not meant to snap. It was almost dark. He drove. The girls watched the road. Mary Ellen stroked Elana's hair. About midnight, the moon rose. *Maishe was right,* Krystal thought. It was an astonishing country. Earlier in the day, she had dozed. Now she sat up, wide awake. Occasionally, on all sides of her, mountains seemed to rise up, at once, as though the womb of mother earth herself were trying to reclaim her lost children. Off to her left sometimes, the cliff ended suddenly. Depending on the moonglow, she espied snatches and snips of great valleys, gorges, rocks, and hills, mountains in bizarre shapes, as though the sculptor had been called out and left the rock unfinished, chipped and chalked, hewn in half-completed angles and miens; then a gently rolling plain budged the terrain till the next queer rock-cliff shape appeared.

It was as though God had chosen this land to experiment with prior to determining what type of formation should go where in the world. One long-range or uninterrupted cliff far in the distance caught her attention. It seemed to go on for miles. The moon hid behind fire-red silver-grey clouds; she could barely make out its outline. When the moon reappeared, she pointed it out to Maishe.

"Yes, I've been watching it too. It reminds me of the long mountain range in *Lord of the Rings*, the one the travelers had to go under in the middle. Strange. It looks exactly like it. I wonder if Tolkien ever visited this area before he wrote the trilogy. I need to research it someday."

So the police officer had been left behind and the college professor, emerging from his latent hiding place behind the badge and off the beaten trail, had returned. It didn't matter. Whoever he was in his many roles and guises, she was devoted to him. He was the one who had come in answer to her prayers to rescue her and take her where she knew her destiny lived. The two and a half years they had spent guarding that Colorado town (how far away it seemed now), hadn't been lost nor wasted nor regretted. She needed some stability for a while. He needed to get it out of his system. She was sorry she couldn't be beautiful for him. She so wanted to for her brave knight of the open road.

She looked over at him. Funny, as the English teacher returned, his age returned. As a police officer, a watchman of the town, he had been young and strong again. As the college teacher, the counselor, he was again old and growing soft.

Rocks and cliffs shot up about her, some almost against the window, then receded. Occasionally, off to their right, she thought she saw a village carved into the cliffs, doorways at and about different levels. Then, just as suddenly there were the open spaces, outlined by the jagged edges of the half-finished rock sculptures. She had a strange image of them being inside a video game, hurtling along a computer-road, dangerous elements to be avoided, the player so far perfect as they—his or her electron wisps, the player's images—sped on through the long, lonely night. She looked at Julia. She was glad they had found her.

They both seemed to like her. They liked caring for her like a kind married couple would care for a wounded animal, a stray destined to become their pet. She could never quite figure her out. But then, she couldn't figure herself out very well, either. Well, it was the way with women. That was all. We are Eve's daughters. We are put on earth to drive men mad and crazy, that's the answer to the whole thing. She reckoned that she and her sisters had done a pretty fair country job of it too. Somehow she knew her craziness was due to the fire. Facing that other fire had helped some. Being rescued by Maishe had helped. Helping him reawaken his sexuality had helped her too. And then came Julia with all her needs and weaknesses. That was it, she guessed. She needed her as much as she needed them. They needed her. They needed each other. It was…nice.

The car continued humming through the night. It's a good thing we took this one. I don't think the Vega would have made it. She realized she was thinking to herself as if it was a conversation, to persuade, who? One of her selves from the other selves? Just as she was becoming rational, was she also becoming insane? Maishe always told her she was smart, intelligent. At first she laughed it off. Then she began to wonder. Now she wondered again. Is that what being smart, intelligent, meant? That one talked with one's self and other selves so much, one almost felt one was going insane? One self? Many selves? If she stopped to listen to the random conversations going on inside her head, she would go crazy.

Perhaps, it was better to be fat, dumb, and happy. No, of course not. She wouldn't trade these last few years for anything, not even life itself. He was old; but he had saved her from herself; what more could anyone ask of another person in this place we are condemned and blessed to live?

They seemed to be the only people in the world, shimmering through moonglow in western rock and desert land. It was so lonely, so thrilling, so American. She glanced at Julia, highlighted by moonglow, subtly outlined by starlight. She liked to look at the girl's smooth female flesh, the little barely noticeable hairs, like fine fur, on her face. She was long jawed, almost like that comedian, Leno, eques-fashion. She had heard Maishe use that word once; she had always liked it and remembered it. Yet she was beautiful in a haunting, thin fashion, Julia. There were four of them now, Maishe's women, she knew him well enough to know that he adored them all. It only had to be female, legal age for his strong morality's sake, to about sixty. That's all he needed to sniff it out. Well, no matter. Scars and all, she knew she was his favorite.

She looked over her shoulder. Mary Ellen and Elana lay intertwined in each other's arms, stretched out, fast asleep the both of them. Let them dream. There was room enough for all of them in her heart. After all was said and done, it was a wonderful and terrifying thrill to at once have the extraordinary power and the odd weakness of being a woman. Julia whispered. She looked at her. Julia's eyes were wide. Her head tilted turning back. Krystal glanced out the rear window. Far into the distance out the corner of her eye, across the vast gorge they had just finished curving around, about seven miles or more distant, she reckoned it, she thought she caught a glimpse of another pair of headlamps careering in the same direction on the road behind them.

"What is it?" Maishe said. He yawned.

"I...," Julia said.

"Nothing," Krystal said. "Just drive on. Can't we go a little faster? We'll see daylight before we get there."

"Krystal. It's tense. I know that. But lighten up a little."

What was wrong with him? So it was true they were all the same after all. And she began to think of a fire and what she might have looked like if—and then she heard the Acclaim's engine whine a bit. It had started to pick up about five miles per hour. She looked about. The women in back slept.

Julia stared wide-eyed ahead. Occasionally, she glanced over her shoulders. Krystal could see nothing anymore except the great rocks and cliffs, gorges and valleys, and occasional rock villages. They fled on through the endless night, almost feeling upon the backs of their necks the hot, wretched breath of a venal pursuer.

******

For a long time, it seemed, she couldn't make out the strange dancing lights in the distance. They twinkled, as if the lost souls in the heavens, with one last desperate measure of light, had sparkled, and, fizzling in a flaming fury, albeit still at a respectable distance, fell to earth. It seemed that the lights sparkled and shone at different levels. Occasionally, the strange corona seemed closer. Occasionally, it seemed to radiate its lights farther away. Occasionally, sudden jutting rocks and cliffs close at a distance cut off its sheen and luster and sparkle completely.

They must be approaching something, however. A few cars had appeared, headed in both directions. Dirt roads off this road now then opened to her view. There was a settlement here, civilizations. Maybe they approached the center of the reservation. One thing was certain. There were two or three sets of headlamps within the rearview mirror now. Poor Maishe. He could never keep anything from her. She knew he saw it in the rearview mirror. After living years with him I know him. We are fools to think he had not seen the headlamps behind us. We are all conflicted. Life is complicated. All seems conflicted.

Pshaw. Look at her, a fire-scarred wanton, thinking hard like that. Maishe always said she was intelligent. Well, maybe she was, after all. What did it get her when all was said and done? Here they were, having stood up to the worst vile scum and putting them in their place for the last three years, and still fleeing some half-suspected evil force like frightened mice. Before the fire, she tasted cakes and mint and laces; she had an elder aunt whom she visited before she was fire-fleshed. Her aunt always served her tea. The aunt smelled of crinolines, doilies, held her two fingers in the air when she drank.

"Pshaw." Actually, Aunt Jules was the only member of her family she could recall being, well, nice to her. Jules. Julia. That was interesting, wasn't it? Maishe told her more than once that there was a destiny in names. The problem was, the mystery of the name, like the mystery of the Great Ineffable Name, could rarely be understood. Perhaps, except for an occasional flash of brilliance and insight, it was hopeless to understand one's name and one's destiny. She shivered. It was a bit frightening. She was starting to think like him. Perhaps it was true after all. Age differences, like all else in this spectrum of the universe, this world upon worlds, were mere illusion. And only three years ago, she had thoughts like a scatterbrain schoolgirl. Now she had such thoughts, she did not believe she could contain them all in her head. Like men everywhere, it was all his fault. And yet…the women in the back of the car stirred. They were awake, and then they—amazing how new love is— you just can't seem to get enough of the other person. She felt her own body becoming responsive. It had been a few days. If only they could stop at a motel somewhere. She looked at Julia and Maishe. Maybe the three of them should have stayed in Hyacinth after all.

They rounded a curve and suddenly there it was, the lights at all different levels shining, sparkling, twinkling throughout this part of the known world.

"What, what is it?" Julia said.

"Look at that now," Mary Ellen said. "Like God's angels fluttering down Jacob's ladder."

"Mary Ellen," Elana whimpered.

"It's a power grid station," Maishe said. "Probably for the Navaho reservation. We are practically in the middle of it."

"Navaho country. It's like, like it must have been even then," Krystal said. "At least out there, where we come through it."

"Pretty," Julia said.

"You have the most gorgeous red hair," Mary Ellen said.

"Like showers of shining scarlet silk."

"Mary Ellen," Elana said.

"Look," Maishe said. "There's a twenty-four-hour Super-Stop. We'll take a pit stop break here."

And there it was, out in the deepest darkest loneliest land in the world, a convenience shop like you might find on the corner in Omaha or Wichita or Tulsa. Conflicts, Krystal thought. The most primitive and pristine of lands; and suddenly a quick shop with neon and fluorescent lights, gas pumps, soda pop, and an immense light-sun lit generator across the street. Maishe pulled into the lot at one of the gas pumps. $2.00 gallon, 85 octane.

"Well, we're getting better. Sorry, Mary Ellen."

They stumbled out of the car. As best they could, they stretched. Some of the kinks flew away; some did not.

"Well, it's a tad might spiffier than my old shop," Mary Ellen said.

******

They bought the snacks travelers buy when they have no luxury of a permanent kitchen, the chips, nuts, candies, gums, pops. They hadn't eaten for a while. They were hungry. They made it their rest stop. Maishe was lucky. He was the only man. He didn't have to wait long. The women, however, as women often have to do, found they must wait their turn.

Native American Indians of all ages, sizes came in and out at a decent clip for this time of day. Perhaps, Maishe thought, *on a reservation, the artificially imposed business hours of 8 to 5 didn't apply.* Many of them, to his untrained eye, appeared full-blooded. Perhaps out here, there was less conquest and intermarriage. After all, in these lands, mercifully, no gold, no good farmland tempted the avarice or exploitation of what must have seemed to the Native Americans a confusing, swarming horde of vanquishers.

Here they were, the true Native Americans and even they had been immigrants 12 to 40,000 years ago. Maishe studied their faces, proud, lined, defeated, smooth, young, old. All with that straight black shining hair. Did they also have a heritage that they too would return to the land of their ancestors—or, in their case, that the ancient land of their ancestors would be returned to them? The Navaho, he knew, were among the most fortunate in that much of their ancestral lands were still theirs. Still, land-rights battles were going on, he knew.

"Maishe, Krystal. I saw it again," Julia said.

When Maishe turned he saw she stood next to the large front window.

She stared out wide-eyed.

"It was his truck. I know it. It went on up the road."

Maishe and Krystal looked out the window. They saw nothing. A pick-up truck (that seemed to be the favorite choice in this community) drove up. A boy and girl laughing and hugging tumbled out. The couple made their way to the store.

They were clearly Native Americans. Still, the flip turn of her head when she laughed, her thin, spindly fingers intertwining the boy's larger flesh padded hands, the clear enunciation of her vowels, his mumbling off to the side, these mannerisms reminded him of countless his students he had witnessed.

Mary Ellen and Elana stood last in line. They sagged under the bags of goods they had been piling on each other, lost to view; only Elana's cascading scarlet curls spewed out over the tops of the sacks of nuts, chips, cokes, juices, candy bars, doughnuts. Maishe didn't know if the car could accommodate their extra stuff. Mary Ellen carried everything effortlessly. At his point, while Maishe filled the car with gas, Mary Ellen picked up the willowy Julia with one hand and spun her around. Maishe had an image of a tree picking up a twig and shaking it.

"Don't you worry none, little sweetness. Mary Ellen and God Almighty Himself going to take care of you."

Elana giggled. She chirped. It suddenly dawned on him Elana's giggle was like the chirping of a robin on a bright sunny day in early spring, when finally one knew with relief the long stupefying winter cold soon would be over. Some remnant of snow might still glisten, but the robin hopped and flew about, the sun caused the crystalline particles to sparkle, a few blades of grass already turned green, and one could hear, truly hear the trill of the chirp. He listened to hear her chirping and trilling her giggles.

She hopped up and down, her improbable ocean currents of bright red hair bouncing everywhere. Krystal looked on, serious and worried. Julia stopped looking worried. She giggled too, deep in her throat and full of emotion. He hadn't heard it like that since the firestorm. He felt well. He felt concerned. He felt a sense of relief. He felt a sense of worry about future days. He felt as a father might feel for a daughter after she recovered from a long illness.

"Time to move on," Maishe said.

"Why'd you let sweetness here sit in back with us?" Mary Ellen said.

"I don't know," Krystal said.

She looked at Maishe. He gave a facial expression, seemingly of non-concern. Krystal knew it was of complete concern. He was, after everything, just a nice guy who wanted the best for everybody and for everybody to be happy.

"Julia?"

"It's all right," Julia said.

"I want to."

Krystal felt a twinge of jealousy.

"Well, all right. But you be gentle. She's a gentle girl."

"Shoot, sugar, we're just going to have some snacks, is all."

They piled in again, under the new arrangement. They quit the parking lot. Within a short time, the sun-lit star lights at ground level, the magnificent light of the great generator station faded behind them, occasionally, twinkling at odd angles in the distance and then disappearing forever, like a parent stands outside and waves to his departing child taking a journey he knows will take the son or daughter far away for a long time. Soon the Acclaim trundled on through now-familiar terrain, through the enveloping night. It was quickly turning toward that deep night when lights faded all through the heavenly canopy, that deepest blackness before dawn's rebirth. All was silent in the car, save for the munching of the foodstuffs.

If it had not been for the distinctive churning of crunching chips, it would have seemed the island of light and goods they had just visited had not been real. Soon the road narrowed. The car tilted, the motor straining. They knew they climbed a grade. They crossed bridges spanning fantastic gorges, only partially visible at night.

"I'd like to see this by day, some time," Krystal said.

"We'll be approaching the north rim soon," Maishe said.

"We could be in our cabins in two hours."

"That's good, I'm starting to get tired."

"Krystal?"

"Yes, Maishe."

"Nothing."

The women in back laughed. Julia's laugh maintained her distinctive girlish giggle that was at once infuriating and enchanting. For the time being the mood in the car lightened. For the time being, the danger seemed forgotten.

******

They approached the park toward 3:00 A.M. There was a long drive through a straight tree-lined row. Then, there they were. The darkest time of night suddenly enveloped all the earth atop the mountain range and the gorge of the river beneath it. As Maishe checked in for the cabins he could already catch a glimpse out the large lobby rear window of that great, glorious, awesome wonder of wonders.

Maishe drove around the parking lot some. He sought out a steel blue pickup, perhaps with Colorado plates. He saw nothing suspicious, despite his old cop's feeling of uneasiness, of something being there when even the known senses denied it.

Well, it would be daylight soon. They were all tired. They were all cranky. They were all a bit smelly (although to Maishe the scent of four sweaty, tired women was still sweet). They needed rest. It would all look better in the morning, under the harsh reality of summer mountain sun. They found their cabins. The small lodges seemed rustic. They had known worse. They collapsed, the five, in a sweet stupor of deep sleep.

******

Maishe could never sleep past 9:00. He tired of trying to force himself back to sleep. He arose. He ambled through the morning-lit paths to the central building cafe, He had an itch to get a light breakfast. He was not surprised to see Mary Ellen performing calisthenics, lifting large stones and logs as weights outside the adjoining cabin.

"Sleep all right?"

"Yea. Best I had in years. Guess that worrying none about that lonesome so-called business is a blessing. Worryin' some about that little girl, though."

"Elsa."

"Yea."

"Yea. Can't blame you for that. Still, you must have some money involved."

"Yea. Well. How much can that ol' sinkhole be worth? Besides, a body can always get money. It's if'n you can be happy with it is the key."

"Julia, OK?"

"Yep. Sleepin' like a sidewinder on a hot rock in the noonday sun. Little sweetness. Right alongside my red-headed treasure, the two of them."

Maishe found he felt a twinge of something. Jealousy.

Regret. Boy, regrets. He had a ton of regrets. He had sold his mother's house, the house in Louisville that had been in his family over forty years. He hadn't wanted to sell it. He was not sure why he had sold it. But he had and increasingly, he found it hard to take. If he had been able to stay in town perhaps. But he had a job to do in his new town in Colorado.

He had needed to return. Maybe he shouldn't have returned. Maybe he should have brought Krystal and Julia back and lived out his days. Maybe, someday, if he could accumulate enough money—

"So, Maishe. You want to get some breakfast?"

"Yes, Mary Ellen. Besides, I want to talk to you about Julia."

******

When they returned to the cabins, everyone else was up. The two of them went for a second cup of coffee so that the rest of the group could have their first, then they were on their way, they split into two groups. They meandered along different paths. They agreed to reunite toward noon. Maishe and Krystal ambled along the eastern path. Soon they stood along the majestic rim itself.

"Can you believe it? It's ten miles to the other side?"

"Amazing."

It struck her, they were like an old married couple, comfortable with each other, knowing each other's likes and dislikes, and what would amaze the other. The sun was bright and crisp, sharper here than in the lowlands, the breezes a bit harsher, the flora sparse but with a harder edge to it. And rocks and pebbles everywhere, as if some giant had been playing with the boulders and smashed them about at a whim. And around every bend, every boulder, any rock, and old gnarled tree, there it appeared like magic, the view, the vista, the panorama, the penultimate great glory of that space of spaces; and, far below, in the distance, one could see a ribbon of a hint of a glimmer of the mighty river that had contributed to the most astonishing of formations on the planet known to its supposedly intelligent inhabitants as Earth.

"Maishe?"

"Yes."

"Thank you."

"Krystal. You are my treasure. My jewel. My diamond. My emerald."

"It's—so beautiful."

"You are so beautiful, standing there looking out at it. A great treasure gazing upon a great treasure."

"Maishe."

"Yes."

"You are charming. It is why I…"

"Yes."

"Why I…love you."

And she was the glory of the canyon, the singing song of the sun, the emerald-faceted beauty glistening off the stones. The breezes welling from the depths of the great canyon swirled above the rim to blow her light frizzed almost shoulder-length blonde-brown hair back from and over the top of her head. It was one of those moments when one could see the girl as she was meant to be, clear, clean, fresh, drop-dead gorgeous, the crisscross patch pattern undetectable, a female atavism, his Eve and his Lillith in one, his own healthy American beauty.

"Krystal. My treasure. My emerald,"

And they kissed there, the man and the woman, this odd couple, over the rim of the great gorge. And they seemed so right together, this time, that no one stared. A tree as old as the river and as ancient as the canyon stood a few feet away, gnarled, its trunk eroded from the center out, but still, like the river, like the canyon, after all the eons, still pulsing with life. It spread its low branches out in all directions. They covered the heads of the couple embraced beneath it. The branches quivered. Their leaves rustled, though it was difficult to discern if the same breezes swirled through the limbs or not.

They kissed for a long time. Finally, the breeze quelled for a moment. The woman leaned back. She was still in his arms.

"Maishe."

"Yes."

"We have to talk."

"All right."

"I think we may be losing Julia."

"I know."

"Maybe if we…"

"She is an adult. She'll have to make her own decision."

Again she was struck with the odd concept that they could be discussing their daughter, not their friend, not their lover.

Still, he was right, she knew, as men and fathers almost always are in such matters. They walked, from one awe-inspiring vantage point to another, from one breathtaking panoramic spectacle to another. It was nature or God the master artist's palette and sculpture, the story of the world told within its rock and empty spaces and they, earth's children, the man, and the woman, holding hands in that most basic icon of deified and human relationships, privileged to be allowed to view the Master's handiwork, His or Her masterpiece. They rounded another bend. Like a nightmare vision, he appeared before them. He stood in the path. He glared. Later, Maishe was to recall, it seemed to him for a fleeting moment the nemesis had horns, a tail, breathed smoke and flame, and, like an aura, seemed surrounded by a red glow. The monster blocked the view, blotted the inspiring visions of beauty and loveliness, all six feet two inches, three hundred pounds of fat-muscle meanness, planted smack in front of them. It was as if he was another tree as if he had been rooted to this spot since the creation of the world, sentenced to bring darkness upon the face of Maishe's and Krystal's light at this moment. He wore the same mud-splattered overalls.

Maishe suddenly knew he had gotten sloppy. He hadn't been looking about, but he knew at once the madman's choice had been a good one. There didn't seem to be anyone else on the path. And it was a mean-looking automatic in the man's ham-sized hand. A 9 mm Beretta, he reckoned it.

"Well, well. Junior. We thought we caught a glimpse of you back up onto the road."

"Maishe Rosstein. The little old bald fat yidz and his ugly scarface Jew-cunt lady. Now ain't this just like ol' home week?"

"We thought you got yours in the fire."

"Almost. Got some scars myself now. The cunt'll understand that, I been gettin' it in my mind that she and me will be lookin' at each other's scars, yeah, touchin' them all over each other and all, soon enough, eh Krystal-babe?"

Krystal moved closer to Maishe. She tried to hold him tight, as though by doing so, she could save them both, as if by doing so she could keep him safe. She knew, of course, that it was hopeless, that it was all over. She knew her life could have no other end but this. She knew it. She knew it would happen. She had known it all along. It had all been a dream, a grand, glorious dream. Now it was time to wake up. Once, she had known hope and light shattering her darkness; now she returned to the reality of being another helpless woman cast deep and forever into the void.

"Oh, he can't help you, none, now. He's the one gonna burn or hang or whatever I want. You got that? Whatever I want? It's gonna be my turn now. I have been planning this a long time. Sick and tired of the day and night you come into my town, mine. And taken it over like you did. And then ruining everythin' besides. I might just choose to put some long scars on him, yeah, how'd that be now, long open scars, set some cotton punk in the cuts and match-fire him up aglow in' slow and miserable. Oh yeah, slut, whore, freak-face, you gonna love hearing him scream from now through a righteous month of Mondays.

"You'll learn to like that, you scarface freak bitch. I'm planning on seeing to it you learn to like it."

"You're a long way from home, Junior."

"What about you, Chief? Can't call out on that police radio up here now, can you? Now move up that incline there."

"All right. But let the girl go. This is just between you and me."

"Oh, she did her part to ruin everything. But I'll let her go after a while. After I've had a few good looks at all the scars and maybe put some of my own new ones on her in all the righteous and proper places. Now—up the incline there. Move. Or die right here."

******

"We're not in Hyacinth anymore, Junior, there's others about. You'll be caught."

"Naw. I got the place all picked up-out behind these boulders here. A nice little isolated space. The wind blowing and all--there's a little cave there. No one'll ever hear you scream. Yeah—I think I'll skin ya alive and cover her in it. Yeah. Some of that plastic surgery, bitch—make you look like a new woman."

It wasn't much of a chance. It seemed to be all he had at the moment. He took it. He remembered his training. Never go quietly to the second place. You may not make it fighting and yelling at the first place; but you definitely won't make it at the second location. Hit, kick, yell, scream right then, right there. However slim the chance, at least it was a chance that would not exist soon after.

There didn't seem to be a way to grab the right arm suddenly and twist it like he had been taught at the academy.

Instead, an image came to him of his high school days, when he played football for a while. It came to him of a sudden, of an instant. In a moment, he felt transported from that high lonely spur of rock overlooking the whole world, beautiful and terrible and free—to the aroma of cleat-dirt divots of grass churned soil, a clean-dirty mud-freshening smell, a stench of birth and a fragrance of death all at once; and the scent of sweaty large young men gasping with gaping maws, gaping with peering eyes, eyes that saw everything clearer then they had ever seen anything. He never saw eyes like that again, until television camera work had improved so it picked up intense closeups of linemen, linebackers, quarterbacks, running backs.

Odd that he would be in danger of losing his life and worse, and the life of the woman he had come to care for more than anyone's life in the world, that he would conjure up the long-forgotten languid hours of football days and the intensity of boys' eyes through their masks. Krystal's eyes were like that always, that intense soul and mind viewing the wonder of the world behind the mask of her stolen birthright.

He stood in two places at once. High off the beaten park trail on a little known, less-used pebble-strewn path on the very rim itself, the wild wind intense and whistling, he gazed out into nothingness, and, at once transported, he dashed downfield after a kickoff to make a tackle, the crowd screaming, the sun bright and glistening; then the approach to the ball carrier and that sweet still moment when all is planned well, mind and body and spirit and the shoulder pads smashing into the stomach and chest, clacking, the sudden exhaled plosive grunt of the opponent, a glottal stop.

He spun. At the same time, he moved forward. He was astonished at how fast he moved, as if the years had not gone by and he was a teenager on the gridiron field again, a time when time itself went on forever and life seemed endless and full of hope. The other two accompanying him on this march of death had not expected his sudden move either, that was clear.

The monster's gut was big, with much air. It reeled with the shock of an immense grunt, as Maishe's teen-age sped borne shoulders crashed into his stomach. All 325 pounds of the ogre hurtled into the boulder at the top of the path. The giant was stunned. The gun jarred loose from his hand.

Maishe suddenly felt like Jack fighting the giant on top of the beanstalk, like David approaching the Philistine in the Vale of Elah.

"Krystal. Run. Yell. Scream. Get help."

He didn't know if he had said it all or thought it or if any of it had made sense; but he glimpsed her running, falling, sliding back down to the park path as he and this monstrosity struggled.

He dashed for the gun, the Beretta dangling in the man's improbably huge fingers. Immediately he knew he had made a mistake. He should have stepped back, drawn the .38 he always carried and emptied it. Then he knew why he hadn't done it.

There was no place to step back to. They struggled at the edge of the world, the most torturous deepest wounds of the earth beneath them. The path Junior had in mind elbowed to his left now, as he caught a glimpse again of the park walk below them. The monster recovered. In one fell swoop of his left arm, he sent Maishe reeling.

For a moment, he thought, *We're not in Hyacinth anymore, Junior.* Maishe looked into his eyes, deep-dark, venal, fell. Then, Junior gazed about. In an instant, Maishe realized he sought his gun. Maishe felt his own familiar piece in his hand. He saw it blaze fire. He felt it leap and jump out of his grasp, as if it had a mind of its own, again and again, and again, till only empty clicks echoed throughout the world, lost in the vastness of the space between the north and the south plateaus. Still, the giant lumbered at him, the monster's right arm dangling and bloody, his automatic no longer there now, but the man heaving down upon him with the size and speed of a steam engine, blocking out the sky. An instant ago, we're not in Hyacinth anymore, Junior. Maishe had been transported through time to an age of innocence and hope; suddenly the world had been reduced to a ridge describing the edge of the earth. This monster was arcane, invincible. He tried to back away. Maishe fell from the earth through the endless spheres of the heavens. Down he dove, toward the gates of hell.

It seemed to him he fell for a long time, turning in the winds and drafts endlessly; he seemed suddenly, strangely at peace, at one with the infinite vastness of the firmament above and with the firmament below, when he stopped to look about, however, he found he lay only a few feet from the top. The entire history of the planet unfolded in openness undisturbed, but for time, beneath him.

He gazed out at all that splendor and emptiness and completeness with wonder. Well, if it was his time to join with the universes, the worlds upon worlds, it was a glorious way to do it. He looked back up at earth. The sky had fallen. A man-monster had taken its place. With one arm, his left, the ogre hurled rocks and stones at where he, Maishe, dangled twixt earth and sky.

What held him? What had reached out from Mother Earth to cradle him, to protect him, to stay his journey through space and time?

He felt enmeshed in a tangle of roots. He realized they were the roots of the great gnarled old tree whose branches spread like an infinite canopy. Only moments earlier, he and his woman had stood lost in an Eden of wonder beneath the great tabernacle of the tree of the ages. Now its roots had broken through the rock face of the mountain, of the rim itself, of the end of the world, and, like a loving parent reaches out to catch with a gentle touch her child as he leaps bravely off the edge of the pool into the warm embrace and the cool water, to cradle him back in its comforting entanglement.

A rock almost hit him. It hit the root spreading over him. There was howling from the man throwing the rocks, a primeval yelling not quite human, not quite animal, and it suddenly turned even more cold-blooded. Suddenly he saw his vision of horror disappear. He heard shouts, yells, sounds of a mighty struggle.

Occasionally, he saw the sole heel of a boot over the edge, pebbles sliding down beneath it, then a bloody arm, then emptiness and silence, Again he looked about him. Eagles soared below him on canyon drafts, white-wing tipped, some with the brown heads of the juveniles, some with the white crowns of mature adults. Smaller birds flew above and below the eagles, flapping their wings furiously to keep up. Maishe wondered why the smaller birds followed the eagles. It seemed almost as if they were pestering the larger birds. He didn't know the species. Perhaps they were—at that moment an odd thought crossed his mind, a strange quote from Willa Cather—"I dream of eagles and I create sparrows."

Deep in the distance, he again thought he observed the glinting glimmer of the river. The drone of a plane caught his ear. Looking out to his left, he saw the craft banking into one of the drafts of the many canyons forming the one grand one. Then he thought, from somewhere in space, from the upper reaches of the heavenly spheres, from above the firmament of firmaments he heard his name.

"Maishe? Oh God, Maishe. He's alive, everyone. He's alive. Oh, thank God. Thank God."

He felt disappointed. He felt joy. He saw the face of an angel peering down from the higher spheres, an angel of beauty and, oddly, if one looked away and looked back, an angel with a strange scar-like quilt patch-like pattern to her earthbound face.

Then he knew it was Krystal. And he saw for a moment no scars nor patch-quilt work on her human flesh. He saw only she, woman, the most beautiful sight he had ever seen.

******

It took a while for the park rangers to work a rope-ladder rig down to him, then for the young woman and the man

182

who descended to discern a way for him to be extricated from his benevolent webroot structure. They didn't want to cut the tree's roots; in fact, when they considered it, Maishe denied its efficacy. The tree had protected him. He would protect the tree. Finally, they settled on a wedge of some sort to move a couple of root-branches aside so he could climb out. They put some gear about him in case he fell making it to the ladder.

He didn't mind, in a way, he was already lost in the reverie of his fall. It hadn't actually been far, he now knew, but it had seemed so and he had seemed to come to know a newer, higher level of being, and being himself. He could sit now or lie down, and at any time he could enter the higher, mysterious realms. *Life itself,* he thought, *is a mere illusion, a whisper only on the wind, breezes, gusts, zephyrs of all this vastness and loneliness.* Of course, he had most thankful escaped excruciating physical pain, the final arbiter of gross reality.

Finally, he was up on the path, returned to the planet of delusion. They were all there, his group, his women, his friends. Krystal ran to him. She hugged him tightly. It felt good to have his arms about her again.

"Maishe, God. We thought you were dead. I thought I'd been too late."

"The rangers?"

Julia stepped up.

"No, it was Mary Ellen."

"Mary Ellen?"

"You'll have to get off this path up here folks. Move on down to the park walkway, please." One of the rangers, the man who seemed to be in charge, assured that his rescued victim needed no medical attention, resumed his authoritarian role and voice. They made their way down. Once safely on the walkway again, they hugged in a big circle, all five. The woman ranger came by. She said he needed to come by the office later. They must file a report. They had already called the Sheriff. He would have to answer her questions too. Maishe recalled he had talked to the Sheriff of this county once concerning a fugitive. Maishe told them he'd be there directly.

"Tell me about Mary Ellen."

A small crowd had gathered. The people gaped at the strange group. But, after the rangers cleared their gear and left, the crowd dispersed. Soon the excitement was forgotten.

The sight-seers returned to the vistas that could never be challenged for very long.

"They were coming in my direction when I ran up there," Krystal said. "I don't know if I made any sense or not, but she told me to get the rangers, and then she was off running toward your position."

Maishe wiped away some blood from Krystal's cheek. She grabbed his hand and held it to her cheek. She was cut a little bit. She didn't know it. Another one of those odd thoughts crossed his mind. *Scars upon scars,* he thought, *worries upon worries.* Still, he had taken his shot and it had worked. He had saved her life; she had saved his.

"I've seen runners run fast before but never saw anybody run so fast like I saw Mary Ellen run that path," Elana said.

"It was all I could do to keep her in sight."

Maishe had a vision of the improbable scarlet curls bouncing up and down along the path, following at a losing distance the powerful runner in front of her.

Elana continued. "When I got there, she was already knocking the guy silly. I don't think he landed one punch. Then I come up. I knew the rangers were coming. I shouted out, 'Holt on to him, Mary Ellen, the rangers are coming.' Somehow he managed to get out of her grasp and slide down that path. Mary Ellen followed but he found me and grabbed me and pulled a knife. But by then we could see other people and we saw up the top of the path, just like I told him, the rangers were coming."

"Besides," Mary Ellen said. "Julia was there by then and leaped up on his back. He threw her, though, and took off running. He was holdin' onto his arm, the right I think, and it was red with blood at the hand. Elsaways, I'da think he might of gotten a punch or two in at me and done our two friends some touchin' harm as well. He run up through that tree line yonder. Ranger said it leads eventual back t'the other side through the parking lot."

"Julia? You OK?"

"She's all right, little sweetness. Just a mite shaken. I'm guessin' we all of us are. I had to stay and look after these two though. So I couldn't run after the bastard. He was bleeding, that's sure. I got his blood all over me. The bastard has AIDS, I could be dead. You shot him, eh? Yea, I heard them gunfires. What's it all about, anyway?"

"It's a long story. We'll tell you about it later. But I don't think we've seen the last of him."

"I'll kill him," Julia said. "Maishe, I mean it. Someday I'll kill him."

"The rest of it, you know," Elana said. Maishe stood stunned in a trance for a moment. Then he realized Elana meant the recent events of his rescue.

"Well, we're all OK now. For now. Let's get cleaned up and be on our way."

"Listen," Mary Ellen said. "You go on ahead. I want to look around a bit more. There's supposed to be a look-out down at the end of this here walkway."

"It's all right. We'll meet up at the lodge later. I've seen the canyon up close and personal. Krystal."

"Yes, Maishe."

"I think I sprained my wrist in the fall."

"I'll look at it. We'll find an ace bandage or something."

They split into two groups again. Maishe and Krystal noted that Julia accompanied them this time. So, after his rescue, after the, what word would Maishe use, trauma, that was it—after the trauma, they were back together, the three.

As the three friends, the odd triumvirate made their way back to the lodge, Maishe looked over his shoulder at the rippling-muscled built woman who had saved his life and at the woman's scarlet-tressed friend. Now the image he had of Junior suddenly disappearing off the rim where the monster hurled rocks at him made sense. She had come behind the giant. No doubt with little effort, she had put her arms about him. She had thrown him back. She had tossed him down to the ground. Then they had struggled, the large man and the large woman. Of course, from the blood everywhere, he had tagged him with at least four, maybe all six of his .38's.

Amazing the two gladiators, this evil bane, this good Amazon. Most anybody wouldn't be stopped by one .38

slug; but anyone should be stopped dead by four or five. *This guy lumbered away; and the woman*—Maishe thought *even with the monster at full strength, not all shot up, she probably would be an even match for him.* Bloody and full of her own blood lust from battle, she seemed to thrive and wished only to continue her day's fare.

Maishe had the idea that Mary Ellen was probably happiest when in the heat of battle and the blood lust upon her. He recalled his intense moments of breaking through doors and running after crooks. They were probably the times he was closest to death; they were definitely the times he felt most alive.

Maishe stopped for a moment as he looked back. For some reason, the women walked on ahead, albeit at a slower pace. He had heard something, like a posse of horsemen on the run, and a loud snort. He glanced up at the tree line. Suddenly, a gigantic white buffalo bounded out of the woods, a creature that Crazy Horse had chased as a penance, a vision quest, a winter's dance of the great hunt. The colossus shook its immense shaggy head. It snorted again. Smoke and flame flared from its enormous nostrils. It pawed the ground. It turned its head to look with one eye directly at Maishe. A baleful eye, Maishe somehow knew that though it appeared fey, its directed harm was not aimed at him. Maishe smelled its fur. It reminded him of the smell of dog fur after the pet had returned to the house after playing in the snow. He felt the heat of the enormous bison's nasal fire. Maishe looked up the path. Krystal and Julia walked on, talking together, giggling, laughing in relief, their backs to him. Maishe looked down the path. Mary Ellen and Elana walked on, talking, laughing in relief, their backs to him. Maishe looked around. No one else on the paths or walkways glanced up toward the tree line.

Suddenly, the sun emerged from behind clouds, rendering the whole scene fresh, bright, crisp, clear. Slight dizziness came upon him, certain tiredness that he always felt as the sun reached its height and arced toward its descent. He looked back at the tree line. Only the trees stood there now, guardians of the rocks, the paths, the grounds, and of the lives of some men and women. He thought he heard the hooves of the atavist at a distance, falling away through the woods.

Maishe Rosstein stood alone on the path above the opening of the world for a moment. He realized he cried. He couldn't stop crying. He stood alone. His tears flowed. His tears fell to the ground, marking the place forever where he had found, for a moment, the answer to the eternal questions. Years later, although Maishe never knew it, a yellow rose grew in that spot, a mountain rose, strange, lonely, hardy, out of place but somehow finding its niche in the pathways of life. Year after year it bloomed. Generations of rangers came to look for it.

Maishe Rosstein stood now at that spot, however. He cried. His tears fell to earth. They seemed to be absorbed, like a beneficial ointment upon a wound. Maishe wondered what would have become of him had he not pulled off that lonely stretch of interstate to fill his tank with $5.00 gas at the place where the spring water flowed at odd times.

******

The rest of the day was spent in the private offices of the lodge. The rangers and the sheriff collected their statements. Once they found out he was a colleague, a law enforcement officer, they were a bit easier on him and his friends but not much. They wanted information. The rangers wanted to be alert for this guy. They made it clear they would like Maishe and his friends to leave as soon as they found it convenient, but sooner rather than later. Maishe informed them that after a night's rest they would be on their way. The rangers allowed that that would be all right. The Sheriff wanted as accurate a description as possible to put out the bulletins.

Yes, Chief Rosstein, she had already alerted the hospitals and doctors in the area. Maishe knew he was being tolerated and the sheriff, a large, fit woman not unlike Mary Ellen, seemed condescending. Well, she was just doing her job, like he had done his. Where, he wondered, did all these powerful, fit people come from? Did the west grow them, wild and untamed? Krystal and Julia sat by him, slim, petite women. Well, what did it matter? A woman was female, that was all there was to it. Mary Ellen and Sheriff Anderson exuded sex in their special way as much as Krystal or Julia did theirs. Once, in the afternoon, they split the group up. Mary Ellen and Elana had joined up by then. The rangers, deputies, and the sheriff interrogated them in separate rooms.

Finally, it was over. They could return to the cabins to wash up. At last, they could rest. The park offered to buy them supper. The park offered to give them their rooms on the house. They returned late that night to the restaurant. They realized they were quite hungry. They dined well on fresh salmon, new potatoes, and sprigs of half-cooked asparagus.

All dishes were cooked to a delicate persuasion fit either for discerning or merely lusty palates. Before they returned to their cabins, they digested the battle over the table numerous times. They collapsed into their beds, all immediately in deep, albeit fitful slumber, more exhausted from the aftermath than from the fight itself. At random times through the night, nightmares jolted each person upright awake. The dreams played out terrible scenes of gunfire and bullet holes, knives and slashings, runs and chases. Maishe's nightmare involved a long fall from an airplane, the Maishe in the dream, which he observed just above and behind him always, desperately, but in vain, attempting to open his parachute. Helpless, the dream Maishe fell and fell…

In each case, the person jarred awake sat in the dark, glancing about the rooms, seeing only those reposed in peaceful sleep, wondering how that could be, listening to the slow, labored, dreary breathing, or the snoring that other times would serve as an unending, undesired alarm. The awakened one then found a way to wipe the sweat from her or his brow, to take a deep breath, determined to lie down again despite knowing the attempt at sleep redux would prove hopeless, and fell at once into a truly deep, uninterrupted rest until the middle morning hours.

Late the next morning, to the unmasked delight of the officials, the gang of five, as they were now called by the rangers, drove out of sight. Maishe drove down the long tree-lined road. He drove out to the state highway. A strange, torturous route through another large state park and some small towns led them through two states, then back into Arizona again before reaching out to cross into Nevada and dive down into the desert.

All along the way, the women chattered but Maishe was silent. Once he caught Krystal looking at him in that knowing way she now looked at him. But, also wiser now, she didn't say anything. Immediately before they hit the interstate, they had lunch at a roadside motel cafe, a normal, plastic cut-out, one among many the same, and they were glad of it. They had known enough surprises. Then they were on their way again.

In his reverie, Maishe recalled he had not told anyone of the other thing that had happened during his long-short fall off the edge of the earth. He had never told anyone of the vegetables and plants that spoke to him. He was afraid they might not understand. He had not told even Julia or Elana, the two people he thought might understand. He certainly could never tell Krystal, who was maturing into Little Ms. Pragmatism. Now he knew he could tell no one, ever. For there, during his fall from earth into space, Maishe Rosstein had heard the angelic host sing their morning hallelujahs—"Holy, Holy, Holy, is the Lord of Hosts."

And he had heard the Earth cry out—"Nay, take not yet my child from me," and he had felt the earth send out her tree's root branches to grab him. Then, there, in that wood-webbed niche of earth, he had felt a hand push him deep into the wood-web, out of harm's way as the rocks hurled down—and then—he had seen the back of a head as large as the canyon itself, with a knot of straps tied at the back, in the nape.

The tree through its roots had whispered to him, "Not yet, Moishe ben Leiv Halevy, not yet; for there still remain many cities left for thee to conquer. And thou must still return, to make thy pilgrimage to the Holy Temple Mount in the Holy City."

Maishe drove on, down toward the playground of Satan, as it were. He felt at peace; he felt disturbed, all at once. For, as he had felt it early in his life, at last, he again felt that he had been born destined for great things.

******

After the incident, they didn't believe they could become so astonished again, certainly not so soon. But the park they drove through toward mid-afternoon that day rose before them with such magnificent splendor, each formation within its boundaries towering to the higher levels beyond the next formation, and it so unfolded, they were again indelibly awe-struck.

Great heaving monoliths, one after another, suddenly heaved out of the land. These were mountains, each one, yet not a range truly, but each with great height and great girth thrust from the land itself. It was as though the travelers westward had landed on another planet, an alien world of tormented, massive, thrusting, pyramidal structures, one in line to the other, as though marching.

As they rounded the narrow road hugging the breadth of the multitude of mountains, snaking around each one's girth in a precarious grade yet in a fashion instilling confidence in the road as well, Maishe espied at a distance, atop one of the far high peaks, a woman dressed all in black. The wind whipped her long skirt and her long black hair. He could not see her face for she wore a mesh veil. Yet, of a sudden, she turned to look at him. Then she spoke. He looked around the car. He knew no one else saw her. He knew no one else heard her.

"You are wondering why I wear black. You see me here. I wear black because I am in mourning for my life."

As they departed the park, their sweet anointing cup of astonishment overflowing, passing through the valleys of these smooth-faced mounted majesties, the ohs and ahs dying down, Maishe realized the other process of the massive monoliths that had them standing apart from anything else he had seen. Although there were levels to the land, and the structures seemed to be resting on some sort of small mountain range themselves, the huge (huge? Gargantuan) pyramids had no cliffs, no ledges, no niches. They were as smooth and clean as the day they had erupted, born from the planet's womb. On those rock faces, there was no life, no vegetation, no ancient trees with roots that could pull a man or woman to safety. In that place, there was no place to hide.

******

Night fell. Krystal dozed. Mary Ellen slept. Elana slept. Julia, as usual, unable to sleep until the hour turned after midnight, peered through the night. Maishe forced himself to stay awake. He drove on through the cool, lonely desert. The woman wide awake felt serene for the moment. She felt safe for the moment. She sat between the two people she loved most in the world, the man and the woman. She had strayed from them. Now she had returned. She never wanted to be apart from them again.

For some time now, she had played the long car chase and the wreck over and over in her mind. At first, it was more than merely playing it over, like a film or a video recording; it was as if it was actually happening to her each time—with one exception.

The highway was not an interstate expressway; it was a long black spiraling tunnel. The spirals were silver lines, glistening in the dark. There was light at the end of the tunnel, but it receded and got smaller rather than coming closer and increasing in size. Then, suddenly, and, in an odd thought tangential to this reliving process, she considered it might be like the inner life of a man in the moments of anticipation and at the height of his sexual orgasm, only with great pleasure instead of fear and dread, as if released by a coiled spring, she felt herself in the car hurled with explosive force, erupting out of the tunnel opening and flying through the air for a long time, then floating to earth, her skirt billowing open inside the cab of the car, then the earth rushing up to pound the car upon the ground with a thud. She felt herself jarred awake at night or jarred out of her reverie during the day. Then her head hurt where she had hit the windshield.

She always felt amazed that the woman in the dream wore a skirt, a pastel-print flower pattern, very soft, quite delicate, clearly feminine. Gradually these moments had improved. She settled into life at Hyacinth. It was better than she could have hoped for. Her life in Iowa was no life. She was glad to be away from it. In fact, she was not sure if it had been her life or some nightmare. In many ways, she felt she had been born that special night of the crash, and the man, Maishe, and the woman, Krystal, had magically appeared to find her in the driving, thunderous rain, to rescue her. She had long forgotten the reality that it was she who had found their car.

She was weak, she knew. Often she found she had difficulty determining if she was dreaming or living in that world others called reality. She had heard Maishe use and explain the word Epiphany once and felt that was what she experienced the night of the crash, her epiphany. Then that monster, that evil devil had come and taken her back to a nightmare. For a while, she thought she was dead.

She thought that she would no longer exist in either the world of reality or the world of her special self, her own secret world. She thought that she would no longer be able to dream her dreams, her wonderful dreams of secret rooms, of large pink and purple butterflies, of the dancing, glittering lights and a long piazza expanse beyond, places where she felt privileged and prized and wonderful just for being who she was. More often than not, she had to force herself to see through the frosted window of this wonderful world to envision this curious and random reality that those in the plane of reality discussed.

And then she knew their harsh reality while lying naked, exposed on the stone slab, while the evil ones who had killed her butterflies, ripping apart their gorgeous gossamer wings and extinguished her lights, smashing each one with a raised fist sleeved in a leather black glove, the affair ending with the musical tones of shattered glass and broken dreams, had their way with her body, imprisoned in this plane of existence. In dark robes and hoods, nude beneath, they chanted redundant half-tone tropes. They danced about her.

Then, with only the others' world of reality left her, she prayed to God the others, in reality, prayed to. She prayed for Maishe and Krystal to rescue her again. Then Maishe and Krystal (sent by the One True God in the others' reality that Maishe talked about some times) this man and this woman, her own god and goddess, heard her cry in the night of harsh reality, came to her, and rescued her once more, as she knew they would.

Then, she knew, her own devil was chasing her again—and this time he chased her own god and goddess. And she knew the day would come when she would have to face him herself and kill him forever. On that day, her day of Epiphany, she knew, her dreams and her weakness and her reality would join to be the same. On that day she would be healed. On that day she would be. That was why the monster had been able to escape Mary Ellen's grasp and Maishe's bullets and lumber off into the woods to the parking lot and escape beyond. The time had not yet arrived on earth for their final meeting. But it would come, and soon it would come, now she knew where her destiny lay.

Then, riding through the desert night, underneath all the stars that could be seen, but upon a great shining star in the east she saw, she vowed a vow. When that time arrived on earth, and she knew it would be at the sand of the sea, she, even she, crazy little Julia, would be ready. She turned to look out the back of the car. She half-expected, and half-hoped, to see the pattern of the two headlamps she could now discern, following at a distance, like a buzzing fly or gnat that always hangs around but can never quite be swatted.

But the only headlamps were not those headlamps. Even the headlamps she perceived, disappeared beyond a hill they had traversed moments earlier. When she turned, they were just cresting the highest ridge before the desert fell toward the mountains riming the ocean valley. A great, long, glistening panoramic kaleidoscope of lights of white and many colors, twinkling and shining brighter than any she had ever seen, a great swelling sea of light, as if a revelation had chanced upon the desert floor, greeted her eyes. Maishe felt something odd. He glanced in Julia's direction. For the moment, he was awed by the sea of sparkling lights swirling a dance in Julia's deep brown eyes.

"Maishe?"

"Julia. You've been up the whole time, watching."

"It...It's..."

"It's Las Vegas, Julia. We're only about thirty miles away. Up here you see the whole thing, the entire city, almost, like an airplane pilot,"

"It's so beautiful."

"We'll be there, in only half an hour."

"It's so beautiful."

"Less than half an hour."

"Do you see the butterflies?"

"Butterflies?"

"It's like my dreams."

Maishe Rosstein looked over at Julia as a father might look at his daughter on a long vacation car trip. He smiled. He drove on through the lonely, cool desert.

Desert

8

Sand

He drove them through the valley of lights. They were again astonished. They had been in awe of nature's great wonders; now they stared in slightly less wonder at men's and women's achievements. It was at once garish, artful, disturbing, serene, obscene, beautiful, outlandish, inviting, alluring, deceitful.

Maishe knew that great evil lurked behind every façade here, wrongs both speakable and unspeakable. Yet he also knew that prosperity beckoned here, so there was good as well. Fortunes had been made in one night; many more fortunes had been lost in less time. There were comedians and shows whose names he recognized; comedians and shows whose names he did not. Maishe made his way through town. Then, in short measure, they were out on the desert road known as the Strip. Out on the Strip, the buildings seemed farther apart. One could see the sand of what was, after all, the middle of the desert, the original oasis long lost and covered up. To this oasis men building the Hoover Dam had come at night to drink beer, whiskey, rye, gin. These were tough men, tough-handed men, big-armed men, men who knew and who meant the business of the moment. These men drank. These men visited the camps of the women who followed them. Then, these men brought an omen of prosperity to the sleepy desert village.

These men gambled. They gambled in their camps. They gambled in the saloons. They gambled in the hotels. The leading men of Nevada, in their wisdom, determined to court prosperity instead of indicting it. Bugsy Siegel had envisioned a vision out here, farther out from the village. Out in the desert, he built the Flamingo. Siegel had been assassinated before he saw how true a visionary he came to be. Now there was wealth in abundance and ruined lives without measure.

"Maishe, can we stay there, where they have a circus?" Julia asked.

Indeed, Maishe saw there was a place called Circus-Circus; the large billboard in front announced they had acts playing throughout the day. They registered for an adjoining suite. They had to go to the rear building, to take a tram to where the casino, restaurants, circuses gambled, served food, spun acts. It was short elevated monorail with cars that came and went about every ten minutes. In a way, it as a fun ride itself. Exhausted from the long ride through the desert heights and its floor, they slept until noon. For a day or two, they meandered about their own hotel. They ate in the cafes and buffets. On the lower floors, they stood transfixed by the gamblers. On the upper floors, they watched the circus acts. They munched fresh and growing stale boxed popcorn. They agreed they liked the trapeze artists best. They came to follow the schedule when the troupe grasped each other's hands and arms a hundred feet in the air, to hurl each other between earth and sky, that is, between the cathedral domed ceiling and the wood floor.

Occasionally, they split in different directions. During these times Maishe tried his hand at small stakes poker. Maishe thought himself a good poker player but he made the mistake of sitting at a stud table. The game moved so swiftly, he soon realized he was out of his league. It was too late for him. He dropped $10 in less than a dollar a minute. Later he found a draw game. He won back his stake and a few bucks into the bargain. *Well*, Maishe thought, *I don't think the eyes in the ceiling will need to worry much about me.*

A night or two later, they did Vegas, hopping from one free show to another. Maishe especially enjoyed watching the topless dancers. The girls looked happy with their jobs. Perhaps, they weren't exploited. He was sure it was very competitive. He hoped they were paid well. Maishe noticed that Julia gazed about, as she had since that day she caught a glimpse of Junior's truck in the distance.

Nonetheless, she didn't say anything. He and Krystal had noticed nothing unusual either. Perhaps they finally were rid of that scum. He hoped Junior hadn't limped back to Hyacinth, though, to begin again his evil small town empire. Not after he and his girls had spent so much of themselves and of their years cleaning up that mess.

As for Mary Ellen and Elana, as the week wore on, they gradually began to seek out a permanent place to live. Maishe watched them one day at a distance. The impossible cascades of bright scarlet hair blew every which way alongside the large fit woman, as though it were the bonnet of hair alone attempting in vain to keep up with the athlete beside it.

Soon Mary Ellen announced she had a job as a bouncer in one of the bars. Elana was looking for a place to set up her practice of shiatsu and reflexology. Apparently, her job in an established spa had been filled. Well, Mary Ellen allowed, it had taken them a bit of time to get out here; but she added that they wouldn't have traded any of the experiences for any job. They were getting settled. Maishe knew it was time to depart.

10

Ocean

Before they left, Maishe took the women to see the cinema at Caesar's Palace. Mary Ellen started asking about the statuary along the drive at once, Maishe tried to tell her about as many of the myths as he could recall. It was like any other skill, Maishe realized—if one doesn't keep up by teaching, reading, or researching, one forgets. The women, however, seemed impressed with what he knew. *You can take the teacher out of the classroom, but you can't take the classroom out of the teacher,* Maishe thought, *not for the first time.*

They had to walk through the now-familiar enchanting soft glows amid the plinks and the plunks of the slots, coins, chips falling away on blue-green fields of velvet, the gamemasters barking out their tropes of enticement, of hope grown full, of hope crushed. They smelled the smells of excitement, anticipation, disappointment, joy, despair, courage, and weakness of the heart. There was the scent of something else as well, a certain indefinable spoor, the same blood lust trail the ancient ancestors must have sensed as they tracked the wild boar for their survival or in stealth crept upon an enemy in preparation for a crucial battle.

Finally, they worked their way through all the seductive folly. They arrived at the theater. They bought their tickets. For a while, they were compelled to stand in line. At last, they were let in the theater. Maishe noticed the crowd here was different than in the casinos. These were vacationing families, moms and dads, and the kids, here and there a grandma or a grandpa, young people on dates—it was as though this theater was a time capsule set to the '50s while all about it swirled the basest of human passions let loose, a calm eye, peaceful and value-laden, awash in a swirling whirlwind, a cataract of desires fey and blissful, disciplined and gross.

The movie was some Hawaiian adventure Maishe had trouble concentrating upon; however, the women and the other audience members seemed enthralled. In a short time he, the old film critic, realized that whatever flimsy excuse for an exposition, a progression, a climax, a denouement was being illumined by the magic lantern upon the screen, it served a mere excuse to show the realism of the domed, encapsulated, sensurround movie effects. And, by gum, he had to admit it worked. You were supposed to sit back in your chair and gaze at the domed screen, while the light borne images casting around the entire ceiling of the theater have the sensory impression you were within the film. The hurricanes, the launched boats, all of it, therefore, seemed to be even more three-dimensional than the old 3-D.

Maishe recalled the old planetarium and the way you were supposed to lean back and gaze at the dome ceiling at the stars while the strange giant insect-like device at the center of the audience circle rotated around, a thousand points of lights peeking through its exoskeleton.

Perhaps because essentially it was, after all, a movie he was watching, it led him to recall the planetarium scene in *Rebel Without a Cause,* with the great James Dean, one of only his three films.

The planetarium director had been represented in the stereotypic dork fashion (although Maishe recalled when he was a child the planetarium director at the Rauch Planetarium in Louisville did look and act similar); but the other characters were so well-drawn, the plotline so fully realized it remained one of Hollywood's great films. They were all gone now, everyone. Jim Backus, Sal Mineo, Natalie Wood, and, of course, James Dean. The three of them—Mineo, Wood, and Dean had died under definite or somewhat mysterious circumstances. Three good young actors who should all be alive today, growing old, gone like the wind. *Men dream*, Maishe thought; *angels in heaven laugh; demons in hell sneer.*

There was another movie like that, *The Misfits*. It was the curtain call for three fine actors—Clark Gable, Montgomery Cliff, and Marilyn Monroe. Again the actors had died under varying and, in Monroe's case, most assuredly mysterious circumstances. There was Sharon Tate. There was that actress in more recent times who had been stalked. Well, it did make you wonder.

A thunderous lightning bolt crash in the hurricane on the Hawaiian Islands created an eerie bright cataract-thump cascade of light for a brief second. Maishe immediately thought of the storm scene from *The Poseidon Adventure.* Julia screeched. She grasped his arm, hard. Maishe jolted from his reverie. It was like the night he had sat bolt upright, instantly awake from his nightmare, only to perceive that everyone else was asleep and in varying fits of light and heavy snoring.

"Maishe. Dear God. I saw him. He's here. He's in the audience. The Devil. The Devil. God."

"What. Where?"

"Over there. I saw him."

Maishe used the lighting in the film, the momentary brightness of the theater to grasp glimpses across the way. He couldn't discern him. Julia could not see him again. But he had come to trust her acuity in these matters. His hand searched the back of his belt, under his jacket where he kept his .38. Yes, there it rested, waiting. Would they never be rid of this animal? Now he was wounded, crazed more than ever, stalking them. How was it possible that such a big man could flit in and out this way? Always he had them at a disadvantage. Perhaps, after all, he was a devil, an evil spirit who metamorphosed as he needed and only appeared corporeal when he felt ready to frighten or to attack earthly entities. God's dialogue with Satan in that peculiar book of The Holy Scriptures came to him.

"Where have you come from?"

"From roaming through the earth and going back and forth in it."

"Have you considered my servant Job…?"

It was another farewell. Again Maishe felt the old feeling of remorse, a regret cherished and despised. He really should have stayed and lived his life in his home town of Louisville, that beautiful northernmost of the southern towns, that jewel of the Ohio River. But he had cast his die years ago. Now there was nothing left to do but see his journey through to its end.

They proceeded through the hugs, the tears, the laments, the promises to write which would be broken in weeks, months, years. Maishe hugged the large woman last. Again he was struck with the erotic fantasies he had envisioned since they met. His head rested with peace between her breasts where it felt warm, cozy, comforting. She always towered over him. He relished it, looking up to her chin, her nostrils, her eyes, her forehead, her hair. *How wonderfully secure it would be*, he thought, *to be a kept woman, looking up at a strong, sensible man who took care of all her needs.*

At once, he saw himself lying naked beneath her, she too powerful for him to escape, to move; in fact, she forbade him even to twitch or he would really get it. He must lie completely still while she had her erogenous ways with him, teasing him with her tongue, lashing him with her wide thick belt strap, massaging his body and his soul with painful pleasures and pleasurable pains. Maishe didn't seem to respond the way most men seemed to respond. Most often, as he considered the ways of the flesh, or began its delectable rituals, no instant erection arose.

Still, more often than not, he found if he concentrated only on addressing his partner's pleasure, things evolved the way they were supposed to. He was too tense, he knew. The muscles that were supposed to relax didn't fully relax, failing for a while to allow the flood of blood flow into the long, sponge filled cavity, raising a limp vessel to engorged proud pointed stiffness. As he found his way through the always fascinating journey of magically conceived beauty that was a woman's body, he lost himself, and the sphincters wound tight, like the shutter of a camera, or the shutting of an eye's pupil tripping from dimness to the bright expansion of light, trapping the wash, the wave, the wellspring of blood life. Sometimes, he even began to worry if, at the other end, the sphincter in its turn would relax, returning the state of affairs to its soft, flaccid reality.

So this was the kind of person he was after all. He said good-bye to the woman who had saved his life while imagining her dominatrix. He was an old man dreaming dreams of torpid sport with young women, envisioning visions of unspeakable perversion with women who had rescued him from terrible fates, unthinkable tragedies. Still, it would be a pleasant thing to relax for a while, to be the one nurtured, protected, played with, passive, and let the dominating one worry about the details. Perhaps, if they had more time…

"Julia, honey, are you sure you don't want to stay here with us? We'll take good care of you, won't we Elana?"

"You betcha." That incredible white-toothed smile, under those impossible scarlet curls. Elana straightened her astray hair. Immediately it bounced back.

Krystal caught Maishe's eye. It was her mother's iconic, worry look. Astonishing how much she had matured from the lost waif he plucked up from a deserted stretch of rural highway. She was strong now. How far away Omaha felt. How glad he was of it. In Omaha, his whole life had passed him by. He knew all he needed was a break of some kind. None ever came. One day he took to the open road. He thought of his daughter and if she was OK. He needed to call her when he got settled in LA.

"Yes. I'm sure," Julia said.

And Maishe saw the sense of relief spread across Krystal's face, even the patch-quilt reality unable to mask the truth.

"I need to wade into the watery waves of the ocean, to spread my arms wide and become one with surf, sand, and sky, to see if I spread my wings, if I can fly like a butterfly, sail like a sailing fish with flying fins, if I can floa…"

"Julia, what is it?" Krystal said. She could detect Julia's moods now, like a mother can sense when her daughter needs her.

"Nothing. I, I just…"

"Is it…did you see him again?"

"No, I…yes…that is, not here but—I'm all right now. Let's go. It's time. I have the destiny to keep. On the beach."

It occurred to Maishe that Julia also was maturing. Perhaps the readings he read with them at night—Aristotle, Sophocles, Euripides, Shakespeare, Chekhov, Kafka, Singer, and others had paid off. Their sense of things, their thought processes, their grammar, their vocabulary, their references had improved. You can take the teacher…

"Well, take care of this guy. I was thinking of stealing him from you and stowing him away as my ankle-bound, wrist-tied love slave, in a place only I know. Maybe someday. I just want to love him to death." And Maishe found himself again gently smothering in the luxurious soft breasts, found himself crushed with hard, fit, muscular arms.

At last, they were off, the three, the old man and the two young women, as they had been since Colorado, skimming the highway west, late in the afternoon of a late summer's day, sailing across the desert. About an hour out of town, they sighted a boat far in the distance, a large sailboat, tilting this way and that upon the sea of sand, and beyond, the boundless desert hills and mountains with rivulets of water or ribbons of sand strip roads running up to isolated villages or ghost towns. Whether the ship was a mirage or a desert sailor, they could not say; but they were stuck with it and it wasn't until darkness fell upon the desert floor and highway that they lapsed into silence, each with his or her own thoughts.

******

About midnight, at the final desert town before the megalopolis that had become L.A. and its environs encompassed them, they pulled in to a Denny's. The company seemed to have its restaurants everywhere. Maishe trotted out the old lame joke about how when the astronauts completed their journey to Mars, and they wished a midnight snack, they would find a Denny's around the mountain, offering a Grand Red Sand special. Although clearly a bit of a struggle for them, the girls managed polite giggles and sneers.

They allowed their meal, snack, and rest to take well over an hour; then they were on their way. Now there was nothing left to do but wind through the web of L.A.'s complex freeway system and, as he had promised himself and the girls, years before, head straight for the edge of the continent to the point where they could drive the car no longer. Soon enough, for there was little traffic this time of deep night and early day, he approached the center of the city.

The buildings, tall and serene, like those of any large city, arose off to their right. To their left lay, the tree-shaded campus of Southern California University, where years (years? decades, now) before he had been offered an entrance ticket to the magic kingdom, and, like an utter fool, had let it somehow slide by.

On they traversed the freeways. Soon enough, they turned on Venice Boulevard, heading southwest for one of the world's famed beaches. An occasional twenty-four-hour restaurant or gas station wearily blinked at them as they drove. For a while, driving through Los Angeles, they conversed. Now, through Santa Monica and on into Venice, they caught the scent of the ocean upon the breezes. The odors, as always, mixed with the aromas of sand, salt, gasoline, and something else, a fishy smell. They sat silent. The car drove on.

Soon they saw moderate-sized but expensive homes, green and azure pastel blocks painted in square arranged neighborhoods. They sat straight now, now they leaned forward in the car's bench seat, eager and full of anticipation to see the great mystery of teeming life itself, the water's ocean, the ocean's water, the great swirling, swelling, swimming sea that served as the amniotic fluid of earth's womb.

They crossed a bridge. Numerous sailboats, their naked masts poking toward the sky-like pins in a needle cushion sat bouncing at rest of the canal below. The homes changed here, turning to large seafront apartments or condominiums. Then, of a sudden, it appeared in the distance, that great undulating tide that brings with it the encouragement of some cares and washes away a few woes, if one stood long enough by its edge.

Again, at this hour, he had no trouble finding a parking place. Within a moment, they floated upon and sank within the giving sand. It fell and rose, rose and fell beneath their feet. Without too much effort, they made the natural adjustment. They stopped to listen to that seething, unique sound, the waves lapping or lashing in upon the wet sand of the shore. Then they dashed as well as they could across the soft sand, lifting their feet out of the shifting sea soil, headlong, to the water's shoal. They had made it.

They commenced their journey in the center of the continent. Now they stood at the continent's edge. The girls kicked away their shoes with their feet bare and their toes wiggling, they kick-shoveled sand. Barefoot, the two women squealed with childlike delight at this most basic and primeval delights, they played tag with the onrushing waves. They were here, just as he said they would be here. His responsibility was over; and his responsibility began.

Somehow he had to find a way to introduce them to people who knew people. He had been giving them acting lessons and exercises along the way. They needed more— profiles, a resume, a photograph, a start in small bit roles, or if they were lucky, a commercial. Again, as a hundred times before, he tried to think of the people he knew in the business. Would they still be here? Would they remember him from the old days? Would they have some influence, any influence?

Then he forgot it all for a while, the entire gamut of playing the game, of making it for his girls, for his women. For a moment, he thought of it, not at all, not even a whit.

For dawn broke far beyond them. He was drawn to its wonder, to its majesty, to its glory. A red glow danced a dappled dance over the face of the waters, daubing the whitewash of the waves distant and near, a tint not unlike the improbable hue of Elana's great curls.

The sea waved incarnadine, lapping a scarlet and orange wash upon the waters of the deep and upon the firmament. They stopped wading. They stopped running into the waters. They stopped running out of the waters. They stopped hopping up and down. They stood, arm in arm, the three of them, dark silhouettes against the rising palette spreading its rainbow far into the horizon. Against the magenta swell of breaking darkness, a solitary white sailboat shimmied up and down and tripped along, then tipped over the horizon's edge.

"Oh, Maishe. Krystal. It's…It's so beautiful just like I imagined it to be."

"Thank you, Maishe."

"Welcome to LA," Maishe said.

******

"Yeah, welcome to LA."

They had been lost in the mystery of the rising sun of the east and its cast upon the waters of the west. They had not heard him skulk through the sand behind them. Maishe recalled that he had not seen any suspicious headlamps in his rearview mirror during the drive along the final expressway net. Somehow the monster had learned to follow them surreptitiously. He knew Junior was a tracker, a trapper, a hunter. He had skulked behind them; or somehow he knew all along where they were coming to first.

It was dawn. They rode through the night. He was tired. Once more, as he had promised himself he would not do again, he was compelled to confess he had let his guard down. Maishe attempted to turn, to secure a good foothold for a kick. He was too late. As he turned, the big man's ham-sized hand came down upon him. It was only because he had been turning it struck him a tremendous glancing blow and did not kill him. He collapsed, floating through the air, like a distant gossamer butterfly in its last dying flight to earth, into the prancing waves.

For an instant, he had the idea it would be good to return to the depths of the sea, to let himself float out and be taken by the sharks and other denizens of the deep that did nature's work. He knew he was stunned. Julia threw herself over his back, screaming, "Maishe, Maishe." Then she was lifted off him, like a rag doll, and thrown down farther in the waves and wet sand. He turned, the waves lapping in over his head. He tried to see through the mist and splash of the rushing, breaking water. He caught a glimpse of Krystal being thrown the other way, back on the sand.

The irony of it occurred to him. Only a moment before they were together, ecstatic. Now, they lay strewn about, helpless before this agony, before this evil, and no one was about. Even security had retired at this time of day. They were alone against the tide. Again it was up to him. He realized his bag of magic tricks was empty. He had to reach his gun. It was the only answer. Junior was almost upon him. His hand felt heavy, encompassed, encumbered, trapped in the wet sand. Finally, somehow (Stay awake!

Stay awake!), he found his holster. Suddenly, his flesh turned as cold as the sea washing all his hopes and dreams away. His heart sank. Again he almost lost consciousness. The gun had disappeared. The weapon must have been lost in the surf when he rolled over. All was lost now. Junior was on top of him, raising his enormous fist, taunting him.

"It's been a long time, yidz. Say good-night."

He knew it was his death-blow. So, this is the way the world ends. There was only one thing left to do. He said his prayer; he pledged to see this monster at the gates of hell someday. Then, the hammer of a hand started down to crush his skull.

At that instant, Junior's head disappeared, and what was left spewed a sea of scarlet and gray and black, with streaks of white. The skull exploded again, what was left of it, and again, and this time, Maishe heard the report of the gun. He lay alongside him now, what was left of his monster's mask of a face, down in the waves as they rolled in and over him, over him, in and out. Three more reports and three more times Junior's dead body jerked. Then empty clicks, one, another, then another, on and on. He sat up. He wiped the water's mist from his eyes. He looked back up the beach. She held the gun in both her hands, as he had taught her, and she continued to fire, though the rounds were spent.

He crawled over to where Krystal lay. She had the wind knocked out of her but was recovering now. They helped each other up. Still, the echoes of the now impotent gun's clicks resounded against the washing of the surf. They leaned on each other. In this fashion, they reached Julia, still pulling the trigger of the spent weapon. Maishe placed his hand over the revolver. He took it from her, without a struggle. Still, her hand made the motion of holding the firearm and pulling the trigger, like one of those mimes in whiteface one used to see at street fairs. Maishe watched fascinated her long feminine finger pulling the phantom trigger again, again, again, again, again, again, again…

They each placed a hand over hers. Finally, she stopped. She looked at them. Maishe saw the look in Julia's eyes he had seen and become frightened of seeing now and then.

"I—I told you I'd kill him, Maishe. I told you I would. I said it. I said, 'I'm going to kill him.' Now I have killed him. I said I would do it. I did it."

"Yes, Julia."

The blood of evil washed by the incoming waves upon the beach carried back out to sea, to the denizens of the deep, from which all life had come. Up the beach, in sand wet and giving dry, they hugged each other, the three friends, and laughed and cried at once, and hopped the waves and skipped the surf and cried and laughed again; for they danced by the ocean's edge, it was daybreak, the evil had been cast out to sea, and they were alive, they were young, or, at least, felt young again.

As they had for eternity, the surf's waves played the beach.

Maishe never again heard vegetables nor plants speak.

The End

www.ingramcontent.com/pod-product-compliance
Lightning Source LLC
Chambersburg PA
CBHW051652060726
47593CB00021B/373